YOU

Loved

me at my

WEAKEST

you loved me series #2

EVIE HARPER

YOU LOVED ME AT MY WEAKEST

Cover Design: Louisa Maggio at LM Creations
Editing: Becky Johnson, Hot Tree Editing
Formatting: Angel's Indie Formatting
Images: Shutterstock

Books By
Evie Harper

YOU LOVED ME

You Loved My At my Darkest (Lily and Jake)

You Loved Me At My Weakest (Emily and Kayne)

You Loved Me At My Ugliest (Alexa and Joseph)

PORTLAND STREET KINGS

Collision (Slater and Piper)

Fatal (Mack and Lana) – Coming 2016

Tail (Della and Dom) – Coming 2016

Pursue (Kelso and Ivy) – Coming 2016

Drifting (Pacer and Sophie) – Coming 2016

Dedication

This is for a woman I know who lost so much. Who fell down but kept getting back up. She fought through her pain for her family that still remained. When I think of strength, I think of her. I dedicate Emily's story of survival through the impossible to you, Donna.

Warning

This content contains material that maybe offensive to some readers, including graphic language and adult situations.

Some situations may be a hotspot for some readers.

1ˢᵗ Man – Petrified, I'm cowering against a wall in the corner of a tiny room. The room is bare. The only furniture is a bed pushed up against a white wall.

The vile smelling man hovers over me, and spits out, "You think you're so beautiful, don't you?" He is red faced, anger vibrating from every pore of his body. "You women are all the same, thinking you're better than me."

"Please," I beg, "I just want to go home." Tears cascade down my face. Fear and torment squeeze at my heart.

SMACK.

My face slams into the wall from his slap and I taste metallic.

The man grabs both my shoulders. My skin slices open from his fingernails digging into my shoulders. He throws me to the bed, I bounce and my hair whips me in the face. The man starts yanking up my dress.

Using my legs and arms I push with all my strength, desperate to get his hands away. "Please don't do this. I don't even know you, please. I was kidnapped. I'm not meant to be here!" I end on a hysterical yell. My attempts to stop him are brushed aside, he doesn't care.

He rips off my underwear and I scream at the top of my lungs. I kick out with all my strength, but he pins my legs down and climbs on top. I'm punching him in the chest and the face as he unbuckles his pants and pulls himself through his zipper. Putting a condom on, he then stares down at me. I stop hitting, breathing heavily, waiting for his next move, to start my fight again.

"I'll teach you for looking at me like I'm ugly, as if I'm not good enough for you."

My eyes widen. I have no idea what any of his words mean. He's insane.

He reaches for my wrists and I buck and twist my body. He takes hold of my wrists and pins them tightly together with one hand, squeezing them so hard I feel like he's breaking my bones with my own. He has me. Pinned down at the legs and wrists. I'm trapped.

He reaches down with his hand not holding my

wrists and enters himself inside of me.

I scream the only thing I want in this moment. The only person who has always kept me safe. The man who isn't here to save me now.

"KAYNE!"

***

12th Man - "Fuck, yes! I'm going to fuck you up the ass so fucking hard, you're going to bleed."

Standing in the room, sobbing, staring at the excited man standing in front of me, I beg him, "Kill me, please. Just slit my fucking throat!" I end in a scream.

He prowls toward me and says, "Well, well, look what we have here. You're not quite broken, but you're close." He rubs his hands together and hisses, "Get on the bed, face down."

I shake my head, tasting the salt from my tears as I bite my lip knowing what comes next. He strikes out and I run to the other side of the room before his hit can reach its mark. My face.

"Bitch! Get on the fucking bed!" he roars.

I look around the room wildly, searching for anything to pick up and protect myself with. I've done this so many times, now; I don't know why I keep looking for a weapon I know isn't in here.

I'm moving side to side as he approaches me. I

have no idea what I'm doing or how long I can run for, but I'm not giving up.

He reaches for me again and I run to the other side of the room.

He turns and walks halfway to me. Then I see it; in his arms and legs, he tenses. He sprints toward me and I run around him, but his arm reaches out and catches my elbow. I'm pulled back with so much force; I'm brought to the ground with a hard hit to my head.

Instantly, he's on top of me and begins ripping my dress off.

RIP.

The shoulder straps are torn away.

RIP.

The dress is yanked down my body. He doesn't even bother with the zipper. The whole dress is wrenched away. He pulls my underwear off and I know what will happen now.

No matter how hard I fight or how much I beg, it always ends the same way.

My body tenses as I wait for the bugs to start crawling over my skin, and as it begins, I do the same thing I have always done. I call out to the man I'm still waiting to come and save me.

"KAYNE!"

***

24th Man – "Sit on the bed," the man says, not looking at me as he unties his shoes and takes his socks off.

I numbly walk to the bed and sit. This man doesn't seem like the others. He's calm and distant. All the others look at me like I'm an animal to be tortured and killed. You can see the excitement in their eyes. This man hasn't looked at me once. I glance down at him, he appears to be mid-thirties, with brown hair and dark blonde highlights and a strong build. Dare I say, he almost resembles a gentlemen.

I stand and take a step toward him. This never works, but my heart and soul refuse to give up, as proof to the words I'm about to say.

"I need help. I was kidnapped. I have a family, a boyfriend. They all probably think I'm dead. Can you help me escape? Please, I need help," I plead; only a sliver of hope enters my words.

The man looks up to me and my body stills; a shiver races down my spine. He smiles at me. A bone chilling, evil smile. He stands and walks toward me. I back up three steps, but freeze when he stops advancing on me.

"Emily, Emily, Emily."

He repeats my name while waving his finger

back and forth in front of me.

"I just found you. You aren't going anywhere."

His hand swings out as fast as lightning and grabs me around the throat. I gasp and try to pry his hands away from my neck.

I can't breathe. I can't swallow. Panic explodes in my chest.

"I should introduce myself. My name is Donovan. We are going to get to know each other very well, Emily. I'm going to be at every party and I'm going to buy you every time. You're now my new toy. I'm going to bring you to near death, and then I'm going to fuck you stupid. Marco may own you, but I will be your master in this room, once a month."

The room spins and my arms go slack. His grip around my throat eases. He lets me go just as quickly as he grabbed me. My knees hit the floor, hard. My hands saving me from face planting the floor. Chest rising and falling rapidly, my throat is dry, each breath in stings. Air has never tasted so good before.

"Undress and lay on the fucking bed or I will really show you how much I hate disobedience."

I rise to my feet on shaky legs and walk to the bed and undress.

"You will learn, Emily, you are a worthless piece-of-shit whore, who is lucky to be able to take my cock. No one else will buy you because they can see how dirty you are. They can see how used up you are."

I don't just hear his words I feel them; they slice through me like newly sharpened swords slicing open your opponent in a battle arena. They stick to my soul and I know they are going to stay there until they seep deep inside and scar me, marring me forever.

I lie on the bed and wait for the inevitable. I don't fight and I don't scream. I learned a while ago, screaming *his* name doesn't help me. He doesn't hear my cries and he's not coming to save me. Even thinking about him has my body shaking with memories of a life I no longer have. A life I will never get back. So I shut *him* out and all the memories and feelings with *him*. Darkness and nightmares are my future now.

***

38th Time – I'm escorted into the room and find Donovan sitting on the bed loosening his tie. The door shuts and locks behind me. Exactly the same thing happens every time and has been happening for the last five years. Although in the past few years, these nights have gone from once a month to one every three months. Donovan is always in a foul mood when it's been longer than one month.

Donovan stands from the bed, frustration coating his features. "Another three fucking months, Emily. What the fuck is Marco doing with you all in that time? If I find out he's selling you to other men, I will fucking kill the bastard."

God, he's so full of shit. I wish he would do it, just kill Marco.

I appease Donovan, knowing a calm Donovan is mildly better than an enraged one.

"No, he's not. We stay at his private house and don't leave. People are following him now more than ever and he's paranoid. The only reason why he had a party tonight was because a new collection piece was added."

Lily, the new girl. She's strong. *Just like I was.*
HIT

Donovan backhands me and my head swings to the right. If I said I was shocked, I would be lying. Hitting and choking are Donovan's favorite things. Years ago, I would have cowered and cried. Now, I turn my head back toward him and wipe the blood off my lip with my thumb.

"As if you would tell me the truth, you fucking whore. You worthless piece of shit. As if any other man would want you anyway. You're fucking sloppy hundreds now."

His words pierce through my numb exterior for only a second before I shut my feelings down and I walk around him and start undressing. I lie on the bed and wait for the inescapable. The same thing that always happens. I sense the sadness and fear vibrate through my body, but have long ago stopped listening to it. This is my life, my never-ending nightmare.

Found, saved, released... freed.

Should I have a smile on my face? I should be happy, right? I'm going home. I'm going to see my family and I'm going to be safe from now on. No more hands touching me. No more bruises to watch fade away from my skin.

But I'm broken, ruined, and worthless. What can I offer them? I'm tainted. Darkness has touched me more times than I can wrap my mind around.

This suburban family doesn't know what true evil is. I've laid beside the devil countless times and he's turned me black. Inside and out.

The world around me grows louder and I come out of my thoughts, staring at the ground. I turn my head to look for Kayne, who is standing behind me. We just stepped off the plane that brought me home. He's watching me, again. Each time I glimpse a look at him, my breath catches. He hasn't changed at all in the last five years. Still the most handsome man I've ever laid eyes on. His wild, short blond hair and deep blue eyes that tell me he's so much more than just a pretty face; his thoughts are always deep and meaningful. His body is still fit and muscular. My head still only comes up to his eye level.

Shouts distract me from my examination. I look around and find my parents sprinting toward me. Across the airstrip not listening to any of the men screaming behind them to stop. My mother drops her handbag, items spilling from it; however, she doesn't stop to pick it up.

Time slows for just a moment as I watch my parents. My mother's short brown hair whips in the air. Her eyes wide with tears falling. I can see one of the teardrops hit her red shirt, and there it sits, a lone wet tear, a teardrop for me.

My father's cheeks are puffing in and out heavily. His arms pumping hard, I watch as each vein pops up as he pulls and pushes his arms backwards and forwards.

I tilt my head to the side. They're running toward me, to embrace me. To comfort me? How long will it take them to realize their Emily is gone. How long until they realize I'm repulsive. And I will lose them, all over again.

I'm scared of their touch. Light, loving, forgiving.

Oomph! They've crashed into me and time sets back to present and harsh reality.

My dad picks me up, circles his arms around my body, and cries into my neck. My mother hugs me from behind. I feel her tears soaking through my shirt.

I'm scared. My chest feels heavy. My heart begins to swell. It expands and the ice around my heart starts cracking, breaking off in tiny pieces.

My mother's sobs turn into screams at my back and larger pieces of ice break off. I'm left with just a swollen heart, who just let everything in. Pain, suffering, torment, relief, love. I can feel it all and it's too much. But I can't turn it off.

My chest starts heaving, but my mouth refuses to open and let out the cries that are now clawing at my lips to let them have a voice. A voice… they've never had a voice. Someone who cared what they cried, someone who would fix the hurt they were feeling.

It's happening. My body melts into my father's. My eyes sting and blur. Slowly, I open my mouth and there they are. The cries. They've gone ignored and unwanted for so long. They are mine. My cries of pain, torment and my relief.

My father jolts at the agonizing sound that's ripped from my throat. My mother stands back and repeats my name on a whisper.

Hands wrap around me from behind and I know whose they are. The one person who at this moment is going to send me over the edge. *Kayne.*

I fall into him, his warmth, and strong arms. We collapse to the ground and he holds me to him. My head to his neck and his hand under my knees.

Kayne repeats on a whisper while rocking us on the ground, "I'm sorry. I'm sorry. I'm sorry."

I continue to let my precious cries go, while the man I love and the man I cried out for so often apologizes for the pain he didn't inflict. Pain I can see he has inflicted on himself.

I'm letting my pain go and sharing it with the world. Now everyone around me knows just how much agony I'm in. And they're listening; they will try to help. They can't. But at least someone cares. That's all I ever wanted.

Moments later, my breathing becomes erratic. I know next my sight will blur and the world will disappear into darkness. I started getting panic attacks at the beginning, before the parties. But I learned how to stop them.

Inhale through the nose, exhale out the mouth, inhale through the nose, exhale out the mouth.

My crying stops and my chest slows. I look up and meet eyes staring down at me. I'm unsure of what to do. I didn't plan on showing them my pain. I calculated the best scenario would be to hide my suffering and move on with them all, with my pain, just hiding in front of it.

Now I'm unsure what this will mean. I've calculated every step I've taken for the last three years. I've had to. Each wrong step could have meant death. Meant someone else close to me disappearing.

I need to regroup. I've longed to come back to my family, but not to hurt them.

I look over at my parents, hanging on to each other tightly. Both on the edge of despair. That's what the devils gave me: pain, torment and despair. But I refuse to share it. I refuse to pass it on. It's mine to bear and I *will* carry it alone.

My plan is to save my family and Kayne from me. I won't taint them with my broken mind and my scarred soul. I'll be okay. I'll be normal. I'll hold them at arm's length and leave them there. It's safer that way. They won't find out just how worthless I am and they won't leave or discard me.

I look back to Kayne and feel his strong as steal grip on my body.

"I'm okay," I state.

We stand and I move away from him. I step to my parents. "I'm fine. I lost it for a moment. But it's okay. I'm going to be alright."

My parents both look to each other, then my mom steps toward me. "Don't ever apologize for being lost or broken."

Tears sear down my face. They see straight through me. My mother's eyes shine with hurt and it breaks my heart. I want to save them. But how can I save them from me when I can't even save myself.

I nod. "Okay."

My father embraces me once again and says, "My baby girl is home."

I wrap my arms around his neck and hug him hard, while meeting Kayne 's eyes.

No, she 's gone. She will never be coming home.

Chapter Two

Standing in my parents' house feels surreal. I look around the large TV room and my eyes fall on the white floral sofas. Sofas I grew up on, watched cartoons on, ate junk food on, watched scary movies with friends on, during sleepovers. Floral sofas I thought I would never see again. I drag my fingers over one of the flowers. A lump forms in my throat. I swallow past it and look up to find three sets of eyes watching me. Each with worried, loving looks. Those emotions stab me in the heart. They loved Emily so much. I wish I could bring her back for them. But she's buried too deep. Under cemented hate and evil words.

"Honey, sit down and rest. You had a long flight." Oh, my poor mother. I had more than just a long flight. I wonder which way she will go, denial now that I am here or wanting to know everything. I pray she goes with denial. However, that's not my mom. She's an amazing mother and wife. She will want to know it all, to shoulder the pain for me, but that's not possible. I'm the only person who can carry around this darkness. *Dirty, worthless whore.*

I take a seat on the sofa and my dad comes and sits next to me. I notice his once dark brown hair is now mostly light brown with peppered grey throughout. The lines on his face are more pronounced and his eyes are sad with dark circles. He stares at me as if seeing a ghost. I reach out and hold his hand. Growing up, he was always cautious of our friends and boyfriends. He was always the last awake locking the house up, protecting Jake and I. I don't want him to feel like he failed. I want to pretend I'm fine so he can take the sadness out of his now permanent features. It's killing me knowing he's blaming himself for my kidnapping.

"It's okay, Dad. I'm good." I try to give him a small smile, but I fail, so I press my lips together tightly, nod and try to convey the lie through my eyes, praying that's enough for him to ease his pain.

Kayne coughs and I look over to him. His eyes are narrowed on me. I could never get anything past Kayne. He's the one person I already know trying to fool will never work.

My mom pipes up and says, "Okay, I'll start on the cottage pie and then I'll whip up some chocolate frosted brownies. Both your favorites, Em." She beams at me and I nod, widening my eyes in what I hope is excitement as my lips still refuse to show any kind of emotion.

"Thanks, Mom."

After my mom heads into the kitchen, my dad stands, adjusts the waist of his pants in an awkward move and coughs.

"I'm going to go and help your mom out."

He kisses my temple and whispers, "Glad my baby is home." Then he leaves the room.

As soon as my dad disappears, I look down at my hands. Rubbing my fingertips together roughly. I'm nervous to be alone with Kayne. He's going to want to talk and I don't know what to say. I know what my reactions will be; numb, uncaring words. Those emotions scare me, but I've been this way for so long now, I don't know how else to be. Kayne deserves so much more from me.

I look up at him and see him staring down at me. "Kayne," I say softly.

"I love you, Emmy," he says quickly.

My heart and chest collides at hearing the words I know my heart has been waiting for since Kayne and Jake saved me. My body freezes as I brace for the onslaught of need I have for this man, but I must reject, ignore and say no to them.

Kayne sinks to his knees in front me. Our faces level. His feelings for me evident in his eyes, swirling like a tornado. I can't just see how much he loves me; I can feel it. The air sizzles with his need to touch me. His hesitance showing with how he's fidgeting with his fingers. Kayne 's eyes pierce into mine, begging me for some kind acknowledgement.

"I thought I would never be able to say that to you again."

The stinging in my eyes now stops as I free my tears and they fall down my cheeks.

His eyes grow soft at seeing my tears. Kayne grabs for my hands, but I pull them away. Hurt flashes across his features and my chest aches that I'm the one causing him this pain.

"Please don't… don't be sad," I say softly. I don't want him hurting. I want to take all his pain away and make him forget he ever met me.

"I can't help it, baby. I finally have you back, yet you flinch away from me as if I'm going to hurt you."

I shake my head not wanting him to feel that way, but unable to explain the truth. He should be flinching away from me. He should be running away from my messed up life and me.

"Emmy, will you come home? The house is still exactly the same apart from some mirrors and vases I had to replace."

Jake told me Kayne lost it and destroyed our

house when he found out I was sold into the sex slave industry. How do I tell him I won't be coming back home? It's not mine anymore; it hasn't been for five years. I wipe my face of the evidence that shows I care. I take deep breathes, build my strength and begin, "Kayne, that's your home now. I-I don't know what you want from me, but you and me, the us…" I pause, struggling with my words, "the us, we used to be, it's gone now."

Kayne 's eyes glass over, but no tears fall. My heart shatters into a million pieces.

"Emmy, you just need to take some time to adjust," Kayne states softly, trying to convince me.

I shake my head; he's not understanding me. Fear crosses his features.

"No, Kayne, you need to understand. I've changed and my feelings for you have changed." *Lie*. "I will always cherish our time together, but you need to move on."

Kayne balls his hands into fists, clenches his jaw, and looks to the side. We stay frozen in this position and in silence for a long moment before he turns back around to me and fiercely says, "My heart is broken, Emmy, broken for having been without you for even a second in this fucked-up life God thought he had to test us with. But mostly, my heart is broken because I can see how much pain you're in. I can never understand why you're doing this to us, to me, but I love you regardless. I always will. Nothing you say will ever have me backing away from you. Moving on,"—he huffs out an annoyed laugh—"there is no moving on from you, Emmy. You are mine and I am yours. No matter how many nights apart we have endured and will endure, that will never change."

I shake my head furiously at his words, trying desperately to hide that his words almost bring me to my knees. They shake the foundation of my strength and numb exterior. I push back hard on the emotions wanting to burst free and show no emotion. Within me, my insides just burned me alive and turned to ashes. My heart along with it.

My poor beaten and scarred heart. One moment's rest it begs from me. *Touch him. Kiss him. Be with him.* However, I can't do that. For me to give it one moment of peace, I will be hurting someone I love too much. Kayne deserves so much more than the whore I have become.

Kayne stands and steps back from me. His jaw clenched tightly, holding on to his emotions. *Reach out to him.* I can't. Hurt him now and save him the pain later. *And yourself, save yourself the heartache you know will come when he realizes how worthless you really are.*

"Emmy, I fell in love with you before I even knew what love was. And I will continue to love you until I'm old and senile and I forget what love is." Kayne pauses, and this time a lone tear falls from my traitorous eyes. "I'm going to give you time and space. But I'm warning you now, Emmy; you are mine. I will be watching and waiting. I won't lose you again. I will fight for you and if giving you space right now is fighting for you, then that is what I will do. Just know when I feel the time is ready, I'm coming for you, for us."

My mouth slightly parts at his determined words.

Kayne walks toward the front door, then turns to me.

"I'm going to move my stuff out of our house. I'll stay at Dom's for a while. Move back home. I can already see how much faking you're okay with your parents is affecting you. Go home and be yourself so you can try to heal."

With those words, he opens the door and leaves. I'm left staring after him thinking of a place I once called home. A house I once laughed in, had dreams of a family in. Going back there is going to be painful. But Kayne is right. Pretending to my parents every day is going to be too much for me. I can pretend I'm okay much better from a distance.

Chapter Three

Dinner with my parents is awkward. During silent moments, my mom tries to fill with what's been going on with the neighbors and my old friends for the last five years. Every friend who married and had a baby is like a knife to my heart. They're brutal reminders of the years and happy memories I have lost. There will be no marriage, babies, or a happy ever after for me. That was ripped away when I was thrown down the rabbit hole, but not into a strange place, into a never-ending nightmare or worse, my nightmare ever after.

I nod to my parents as they talk and smile over at me as if I am a miracle from God. I understand why. Their long lost daughter has returned. I wish I could be happy I am home, but everything around me reminds me of what I've lost, what was ripped away from me. My innocence, dignity and my soul. Scarred and irreparable, there's no going back. I am a shell of a woman and I'm destined to sit across from the people I love, act interested and happy, and nod when all I can see are *their* faces taunting me. Telling me I'm used, telling me I'm worthless. I was once good enough for this family, but now I'm dirty, and if I stay, I will only stain them with my nightmare. I need to tell them I'm not staying here for more than one night. *It's best this way.*

"Kayne's going to stay at Dom's for a while so I'm going to move into his house until I can find something permanent," I blurt out quickly before my mom can start talking again.

My parents freeze with their forks hanging in the air, staring at me. I watch as they slowly process my words and their shoulders and hands start to relax.

"Honey, that's your house too," my mom replies softly as she begins eating her food again.

"Oh, um, yeah, I know," I lie, not wanting to have this conversation with them.

They both nod slowly, looking confused, but neither of them push me on the subject.

"Always a room for you here, baby," my dad states and resumes eating.

After dinner, I head up to my old room and sit on the old single bed with the outdated purple comforter that matches the faded lilac-colored walls. The walls still hold the marks from where I stuck pictures up of Kelly Slater and Leonardo DiCaprio. I was obsessed with *Romeo and Juliet*. I would watch Leo and Claire die over and over again. I forced Kayne to watch it once. I was seventeen and my parents were with Jake at an away football game. I talked Kayne into coming over for the weekend. He was hesitant. Saying if my parents found him there when thcy were away, it would make proving to them he was good for me that much harder. But I was seventeen. I didn't care about my parents. All I cared about was the love of my life, so I talked Kayne into it, and it turned out fine. My parents weren't the type to come home early. They had timetables and routines they always stuck to.

"Let's head up to my room and watch 'Romeo and Juliet'," I say to Kayne. I stand from the couch and pull on his hand.

Kayne groans. "Emmy, no way." He yanks me down and twists us. Suddenly, I'm below him. "I'm not wasting a weekend alone with you watching a sappy movie where they die in the end." He kisses me and I shake my head away from his lips, laughing.

I gasp out in fake horror. "Kayne, that story isn't sappy. It's a life changing epic, love story. And they don't just die! They die for each other. They couldn't live without the other. It's powerful and beautiful and you haven't seen the Leo version yet. You've only watched the older version at school. This version has gunfights and explosions." I stick my bottom lip out and beg him with my puppy dog eyes.

He groans and kisses my pouty lips. "Goddamn it, Emmy, will a day come when I can ever say no to you?" He looks at me as if wanting a serious answer to the question.

"God, I hope not. It would mean I'd have to start buying extra chocolate, extra ice cream and clean my own car."

Kayne laughs out loud and I take the opportunity to jump up from the couch.

He smacks my ass and says, "Fucking too cute for your own good."

I wink at him over my shoulder and he jumps from the couch at me. I squeal and run up the stairs to my bedroom. I'm in my room when Kayne catches me and tackles me onto my bed. He tickles my ribs and I lose it and start laughing and snorting until no sound is coming from me, and my breathing starts to struggle. Kayne see's my limit and stops. My chest rises and falls heavily as I catch my breath.

A quick laugh bubbled up from my chest one

31

last time and I push Kayne's hands off my waist to set the movie up on my TV.

After it's set up, I walk back to my bed and see Kayne lying on his side with his hand holding his head up smirking at me. I smile back at him, wondering how I became so lucky to have him care about me. Love me.

I lie in front of Kayne and curve my body into his. He pulls me in closer, kisses my neck, and wraps his arm around my waist and that's how we stay through the whole movie.

That's how Kayne and I were all the time. So in love. We were always like that even up until I was kidnapped. We fought, but it was mostly jealousy. Kayne and I were both very jealous people. Our love was fierce and that fierceness leaked into our protectiveness over our relationship. We both knew neither of us would ever betray nor jeopardize what we had. But we also knew others were jealous of what we had and often tried to come between us. Despite that, we always came out stronger and on top. The Emily and Kayne team were the winning team as long as we were together.

But not anymore. Kayne needs to realize that, and he will. If he gets too close, he will see just how defiled I am.

I find some pajamas my mom must have left on

the bed earlier. I change into the flannel pants and singlet top. Looking down at myself and then around the room, my stomach clenches. So much as changed in just a matter of days. I pray I don't go to sleep to wake up and realize this is all just a dream.

My mom chooses that moment to walk in and reinforces this is indeed reality and I am finally free. Well, of the guards and rules anyway.

She smiles over at me and it's a small smile. My chest tightens. She's nervous and she should be. What she wants to know from me would send her to an early grave. That's why I will carry my nightmares and memories with me until my dying day. No one can know what happened to me. No one can know I was raped, abused, demoralized, held to the brink of death and then brought back, all in the name of power, greed, and sick fuckers who could only get off if they were choking you while they fucked you. No one can find out just how truly bad it was.

"Em, honey, can we talk?"

I nod, not trusting my voice right now. I want to scream to the heavens how unfair my life is. Why me? Why did this have to happen? I want to crawl into my mother's arms just like when I was a little girl and I had a bad dream. I want her to tell me everything is going to be okay. I want to call her mommy, have her kiss my temple, and rock me to sleep. But I can't. I have to live with these feelings and thoughts—*nightmares*—for the rest of my life. Just that thought alone has me wanting to slice my skin open and crawl out of my body.

We take a seat on the bed and she asks, "Can you tell me what happened, Emily?"

My brave mother asks with a strong voice, yet the tears pooling in her eyes show the agony she fears will come with my answers.

My palms sweat as fear courses through my body. I want to tell my mother just enough to satisfy her need to find out how damaged I am. However, I'm scared my dam will break and I will destroy us both with my memories. I draw in a slow breath and start at the beginning. "A man said he was lost. He wanted to show me a map of where he was going and asked if I could show him where he was on the map. I went to his car and he pulled a gun on me. I ran but he caught up to me and hit me on the head with his gun."

My mother's hand slaps over her mouth as she gasps. I take her hand away from her mouth as tears fall down her face.

"It's okay. I was seen by a nice doctor and only had a bruise from the hit."

What I don't tell my mother is that I didn't see a doctor at all and I was in and out that whole time.

I have no memory of how I was taken to Columbia, who was with me or what was done to me.

My mother gives a hesitant nod. I can see how desperately she wants to believe my lie.

"Then?" Mom asks me gently.

"I was taken to a man named Marco who told me he owned me and that I was the first piece in his collection. At the time, I had no idea what any of it meant, but I soon found out." I pause, gauging how my mom is doing. Her eyes are slightly wider than a moment ago and her lips are pressed together. Her small hands balled into tight fists.

"Around two months into my kidnapping, I met three women; Allison, Donna and Kelly. We were moved to a house in the Colombian jungle. Marco said it would be our home. Once a month, we were taken to a private location and put on a stage. We were auctioned off to the highest bidder for the night."

My mother stands from the bed and walks to my old empty dresser in the corner of the room. She holds tight to the corners and a cry is released from her lips.

I stand from the bed, wanting so much to reach out to her, comfort her, but my hands stay firmly placed at my sides.

"Mom, please," I beg. "Please don't be upset.

Most of the time I wasn't bought by anyone." *Lie. I was bought every time.*

She calms and looks over at me. "And the times you were?"

My stomach rolls and my heartbeat suddenly feels heavy. "It was unpleasant, but it's over. I'm home now. Can we please focus on that and stop delving into the past. I understand you need to know, but look at me. I'm fine." I extend my arms out to show her my physical appearance is unharmed. "I'm healthy and I am home."

"Your eyes, Em, they're blank and that scares me so much. Every expression that has graced your face since the airport has been fake. Don't think I don't know. I'm your mother. You may think you are hiding your pain and misery well, but you aren't. It screams off you like a volcano about to erupt."

My head jerks back and my heart races. I'm not expecting her reply at all. She can see straight through me. I can't even protect my family from that fucking collection.

"I'm not going to push you, Em. I just need you to know I am here for you. I'm here to take the burden from your shoulders. Give it to me, baby girl, so you can get some rest," she says on trembling lips.

"I can't," I whisper in a shaky breath.

Doesn't she understand if I tell her, the burden will only grow heavier? I can't bring this pain to my family. I need to save them from it.

As much as I can't go back to that girl from five years ago, I'm desperate for them to go back to the place in time when they were happy, knowing their daughter was okay.

I will make them believe that. I will give them the relief they deserve.

I will find myself or die pretending I'm okay.

Chapter Four

I open my eyes and look around the room. Straight away, I clench my eyes closed tightly. *Not this dream again.* Tears pool behind my closed eyes and I will myself to wake up. The knock comes on the door like it always does, and then I hear my mother's sweet voice tell me to wake up for school.

"Em, are you awake? Your father and I are having breakfast. Will you come down and join us."

My wet eyes fly open and I sit up ramrod straight in bed. I look around wildly. *They aren't the words my mother always says in this dream.*

"Em, honey, are you okay?" Mom asks as she walks into the room toward me. I look up at her and then I remember. *Jake. Kayne. I was rescued.*

I curl my fingers into the comforter at my chest and lower my chin. A guttural sob rips from my chest as I realize this isn't the ill-fated dream I've had for the last five years. This is real. My mother places her hands on my shoulder and I scream out a cry at having another piece of reality prove to me that I am safe.

"Emily." My mother whispers my name in a tortured voice.

I hear my dad before I see him, his heavy footsteps enter my room.

"Kenny, I don't know what's wrong. She's shaking badly," my mom says in a panicked voice. *I'm shaking?*

My dad picks me up and puts me in his arms. I heave in and out trying to calm myself, failing miserably as the feel of my father's arms sends me spiraling into another sob. They're comforting, loving arms. I've dreamt of these moments for so long yet they never came. Nobody saved me in the moments that took the most from my heart and soul. I want to scream at them and ask where they were. I want to demand they explain why they didn't find me in time to save Emily. She needed them. She needed someone. And now she's gone. *They looked. They tried. They did eventually find you.* Not soon enough.

Please, God, don't take this away from me again. Don't let them see me for who I have become.

While trying to calm my breathing, I hear the doorbell and my mother races from the room to answer. A moment later, thundering footsteps are running through my parents' house. I look up and watch Kayne race into my room. His eyes find mine immediately. My heart squeezes tightly when I see the agony cross his features. Why won't he stay away? I'm only going to keep hurting him.

My body relaxes and I calm as my father gently whispers, "Breathe, Em, Breathe," in my ear.

I hiccup once and whisper to my father, "I'm sorry, Dad. I thought I was dreaming. When I realized it wasn't a dream…"

I'm not able to finish. My father's chest expands and a broken sob erupts from his mouth. He squeezes me painfully tight and then places me on the bed, leaving the room without another word or look in my direction.

My mother comes to me, sweeps my dark brown hair behind my ear, and kisses my temple.

"This will get better, Em. I promise."

She leaves the room and I know she's going to find my father. They need each other right now. More hurt to the ones I love and it's all my fault.

After I watch my mom leave, I find Kayne standing at the window. Bent forward with his shoulders slumped, he's holding himself up by his clenched fists. Head down, he looks defeated.

God, I love him. He's here again, the next day, early in the morning. *Touch him.* With these filthy hands? No.

He sighs and then turns his body toward me. "You need to come home. We both need to be at home. I want to take care of you. I want to be the one who holds you when you need it."

My breath quickens and my heart double beats at the thought of waking up in Kayne 's arms. Heaven. *Until he sees what you have become. Used. Worthless.*

"Kayne," I say and shake my head.

"I don't want to push you, Emmy. But fuck, I need you." My heart breaks at his words. "Going to bed last night, knowing you are in the same fucking town as me. Not being able to see you, have you at home with me, in bed with me. It killed me, Emily. How am I supposed to survive that every night?"

My chest collapses in. How much more can I take?

My pulse speeds up as anger bubbles inside me. Rage at Marco and the men who did this to me. They turned me into this person. Someone who can't have what she wants.

I move out of the bed and run my hands roughly through my hair.

"Why are you doing this to me?" My chin trembles and I inhale deeply and continue. "It's been five years since you've seen me. I've been touched a million times in that time. Is that what you want? A whore for a girlfriend, because that's what I am, Kayne. A whore!" I end with a shout.

Kayne 's eyes widen and his head jerks back as if he was just struck.

"What. The. Fuck," he angrily whispers. "Why the hell would you call yourself that, Emily?"

Is he blind? No. He just sees the old Emily. "Wake up, Kayne. The Emily you knew is gone. I'm used, worthless, pathetic, defiled. You will see in time how tainted and revolting I truly am now."

I ramble off every name I've ever been called. Do I believe I am these things? I don't know. But what if they are right? What if I am those things? Those names are always there, in my head, banging on an invisible door. Never ending knocking and reminding me it's possible.

I flinch as Kayne roars, "Stop!" He punches a hole straight through my faded lilac-colored bedroom wall.

My parents race into the room.

"What the hell is going on?" My dad shouts at both Kayne and I.

My head shoots to Kayne and with my eyes, I

beg him not to tell my parents my true feelings about myself. I know he understands when he shakes his head, removes his hand from inside the wall, and says, "I need to go." He sighs heavily and looks to the hole and then to my parents. "I'm sorry. I'll come round later on and fix it up, Ken."

My dad gives Kayne a sharp nod.

Kayne shakes his wrist and begins rubbing his knuckles. "I moved my stuff to Dom's. The house is free for you to move into now." He reaches into his back pocket and pulls out a black square device. He throws it on the bed, points to it and says, "Keep this on you. When I call, pick up. I mean it, Emmy. Pick. It. Up. I went five years without hearing your voice. I won't do another day. Do you understand?" His eyes pierce mine. His face shows determination, but his eyes display just how devastated he is at my words.

I press my lips together and nod in agreement. Kayne leaves the room, and a few seconds later, we all hear the front door slam closed.

"Emmy, what was that about?" Mom asks.

"Kayne wants us to be together again. I said no. He didn't take it well. It's done. We are done. I'm going to change and then can you please drive me home? I want to settle in and start moving on with my life." My voice is devoid of any emotion. Setting my feelings to numb right now is the only way I will stop myself from running after Kayne and begging him to love me anyway. Promise never to leave me when he sees how vile I really am.

"Oh, okay, sweetie, have some breakfast first and then I will drive you over." With that, my parents leave the room and I wipe the memory of their concerned looks from my mind.

Day two and I'm failing already. I have to do better.

Chapter Five

After breakfast, I say goodbye to Dad and he tells me he'll be over tomorrow to check up on me. I give him a kiss on the cheek and squeeze him with a big hug. He's a good Dad, the best.

When I was eighteen and Kayne was twenty-one, my father found out we were dating and tried to separate us. For a moment in time, I honestly thought I hated him. Now I realize he's just a really good dad. He was wrong to try to keep us apart, but I understand so much more now. My dad hated Kayne 's parents and everything they stood for. They were drug dealers and drug addicts. Dad was always very protective of me, and when it came to Kayne 's parents, Dad always made sure Kayne 's friendship with Jake and I wasn't leading us into his life.

But as much time as Kayne spent at our house growing up, my dad didn't know him at all if he thought Kayne would ever lead me and Jake down a dangerous path. If Dad had looked hard enough, he would have seen a boy desperate for the approval of a man who wasn't even his own father and a family he so desperately wished was his own.

That's the only time my father and I have been at war, and it didn't last long. Three months and he finally saw how much Kayne loved me. And I think he realized he had missed Kayne 's attempts at looking to him as a father figure. When he realized Kayne was looking to him for his approval in almost everything in life, he released his grip on me and we were all happier for it. I also think he started seeing me for the woman I had become and not as his princess anymore, not that he would have ever admitted it though.

I wish I could protect my father the way he protected me.

"Em, one more thing, do me a favor?" I narrow my eyes slightly, waiting for his next words. "Give some more thought about Kayne. He adores you more than the ground loves the rain and sunshine. It might be too early for you to decide on what you want, but don't just throw away the relationship. Think about starting again as friends. I have no doubt your feelings will grow for Kayne again."

I drop my eyes to the ground and say, "Okay, I'll think about it." Not wanting to look at my dad while I lie to him.

He will see in time. I'm doing what's best for Kayne.

Dad gives my mom a quick peck while I climb into her car. Before I know it, she's in the car and we are driving silently through the streets to my old house.

The driveway comes into view and my heart palpitates. I hold my breath as we turn into the driveway, and there it is. The two-story, light blue timber house with the same beautiful white porch.

My mom drives up the brown, stamped-concrete driveway. We pass the white fence that reaches all the way around the house and the many tall trees around the property. The grass is bright green and looks freshly cut.

Mom stops the car right in front of the house. There is no garage here. Kayne and I thought we could add it later on.

I stay seated in the car while Mom gets out and walks to the first potted plant and pulls the key out from its hiding place. I watch as she enters the house, but I still don't move. I just stare at the house. It looks exactly the same, as if no rain or wind has touched it since I was last here.

I open the car door and slowly step out. My heart beats harder with each step I take up the stairs to the porch and then into the house. *My house.*

I look around and it's exactly the same. Just as though five years haven't passed. As if my dark memories are only nightmares I had the night before.

I'm in the entry hall. To my left is the living room, and in front of me are the white railed, wooden stairs to the second level. I look to my right and find the dining room, still with the same round wooden table with blue seat cushions. Kayne and I picked out that table together. He wanted black cushions I wanted blue.

"Black will go with the leather lounges, Emmy," Kayne informs me.

"But black won't go with the rug we are going to buy for the dining room floor. Plus the placemats and the tea towels, which will all be in blue as well," I reply.

Kayne's eyes widen.

I quickly explain my reasoning. "We need something other than black, big man. Blue will lighten the feel of the house. And it's still a boy color and it's my favorite color as well." I hold Kayne's eyes and lift my chin to show my determined face.

Kayne blows out a long breath. Then suddenly he grins at me, picks me up and a surprised squeal comes from my mouth.

"Well, if its your favorite color, we'll paint the whole house blue."

I look into his sparkling eyes and smile. This right here is heaven. In the arms of the man who would do anything for me. Even paint our house blue.

"Em." My mom's voice pulls me from my memories. I tear my eyes from the table to her. "You all right, honey."

"Yeah, Mom, I'm okay," I say softly with a nod.

I walk into the living room and glance over the wooden floor to the two black leather sofas and a wooden TV unit with the same TV and a wooden coffee table.

The framed photographs on the wall haven't changed.

Kayne 's party when he finished his time in the Marines.

Kayne and I dressed for my prom.

Our first date. Kayne took me to the local golf course at night. He set up a picnic under a tree with fairy lights. It was the most beautiful thing I had ever seen.

My high school graduation.

Me in a bikini. One of the many times we went with friends swimming in Valley Creek.

Kayne and I standing in front of this house on the day we signed the papers and bought our first home. The house we were going to bring our family up in.

A ringing sounds in my ears and I feel light headed. I'm going to fall apart. I grab on to the sofa to hold myself up.

I need to be alone.

I breathe deeply and pull myself somewhat together. Enough to be able to ask my mother to leave.

I turn to her and see she is watching me intently. "Thank you. I might have a nap. I'll call you tonight, Mom, okay?"

I'm not sure what my mother sees, but she doesn't argue about staying. *Thank God.*

"Okay, honey, I will leave you to settle in. Talk to you tonight." She hugs me tightly, walks to the door, and closes it behind her.

I just stare at the door. It's painted light blue with glass in the center of the top half. Thick glass is used so you can't see in or out of it.

Suddenly, tasting salt on my lips, I'm brought out of my stare down with the door. I turn into the living room and examine every single photograph again. *Why am I doing this to myself?*

I slap my hand over my mouth to try and stop the onslaught of cries trying to escape through my mouth.

I head for the stairs. I want to break down. I need the shower. If I cry in the water, then they aren't real tears. They will mix with the spray and then they won't count.

I remember everything like it was yesterday. Up the stairs, turn right, pass the spare room with a double bed and white curtains. The toilet straight ahead at the end of the hall and the bathroom to the right. The next room on the left was mine and Kayne 's and it has an ensuite, I choose the ensuite, I want to close as many doors behind me to shield myself from the outside world.

I enter the room and close the door. My breathing accelerates as again I feel like I've gone back in time; it's exactly the same.

White ceiling, pale blue walls, two small glass windows above the king-size bed. Two white bedside tables with a glass lamp on each side. A large bay window to the right of the bed with a window seat. The white lace curtains still pushed to the side. I search my mind for the last moment I had in this room to remember if they were open on that day. I can't find the memory; there're too many bad ones clouding the few precious memories I have left.

My eyes swing to the left and they catch on something on the bed. I inhale sharply. It's my old *Romeo and Juliet*. I step toward the bed slowly and with shaking hands I pick up the play. Something falls out of it. Picking it up, I find a pressed rose, my pressed rose. *My rose.* Kayne gave me this rose at my prom. He placed it on my wrist and whispered, *"I love you, Emmy. One day I'm going to put a ring on your finger instead of a rose on your wrist."*

I wore my rose all night. Through our slow dances and stolen kisses hiding from the teachers. I wore it when we made love for the first time, out under the stars alongside the Mississippi. I pressed the rose the very next day, knowing I wanted to keep it forever.

Ecstasy, that's the only way I can explain it. Ecstasy travels through my body at a rapid speed. All my friends told me the first time would hurt, but I feel no pain. All I feel is alive. As if I've never lived a day in my life, until I felt this beautiful, rare, delicious feeling running through my body.

"You okay, beautiful?"

I open my eyes to find the love of my life starring down at me. Kayne. I give him a grin and he swoops down and attacks my lips. This type of kiss is one of my favorites. I love it when he kisses me as if I'm his reason for living.

He breaks our kiss and pulls out of me. We dress and he scoops me up into a bone-crunching hug. "I love you, Emmy. Only you. Forever."

I sigh into his arms. He's perfect.

"I love you, too, Kayne. Nothing will ever come between us. It's you and me against the world. Forever."

He holds me close and I stare at the rose on my wrist with my hand flat against his chest, thinking how lucky I am.

One lone tear falls and splashes on my rose.

Something is still wedged between the pages of my book. I flip through until it stops at what's sitting within the pages of the greatest love story ever told. A necklace. It has a silver chain with a glass orb, filled with what looks like rose petals. My rose petals.

On the page, where the chain is nestled, these words are now highlighted.

"For never was a story of more woe than this of Juliet and her Romeo."

I close the play and with one hand, I clutch the book and necklace to my chest. Lost and staring at my pressed rose, I slowly sink to the carpet as my legs can no longer hold me up.

Tears silently fall as I continue staring at a piece of history that held so many possibilities for me. A girl who had the world at her feet. This pressed rose represents who I was and a moment in time where I was perfect and untainted.

A life, a wonderful life which was ripped away from me. Taken by the devil, and in return, all he gave me was a broken mind and soul. Scars to bring back to my family and destroy them with.

I hate Marco. I hate Donovan. I hate them all! I hate this world and the me they created.

I lay my body on the floor, releasing uncontrollable sobs. They crawl from my shattered heart and out my mouth into the world around me. And the one thing that makes me cry the hardest is that there is nothing anyone can do to give me back my life.

I hear banging. I lift my head only to groan at the stiffness of my neck. I stretch out and find it's because I'm lying on my bedroom floor. I look around and realize I must have fallen asleep crying.

The knocking continues, making me more alert. Looking at the clock, it's three in the afternoon. I'd slept for almost five hours.

I quickly walk out of the room and down the stairs. Peering through the window in the dining room, I find Kayne standing at the door, staring at it as if he's about to tear it off its hinges. *What's he doing here?* I didn't think he would want to see me so soon after this morning's disastrous conversation.

I watch as he fishes out some keys from the back pocket of his jeans and puts them in the front door. He opens the door and storms inside. He looks into the lounge room, then to the dining room, completely missing me to the side, behind the curtain.

"Emily," Kayne shouts.

What is he doing?

He runs up the stairs two at a time. I walk out from behind the curtain to the bottom of the steps and hear him yell through the house again.

"Emily!" His voice is panicked and my heart hurts thinking Kayne is scared.

"Kayne!"

I hear him running and then he appears at the top of the landing breathing heavily.

His face is pale and his eyes are wild. "Fuck," Kayne says as he shakes his head and thumps down on his ass at the top of the steps. He drops his head into his hands, and after a moment, his booming voice echoes through the house. "Fuuuuck!"

He looks up at me, places his right hand over his heart and says with a tremble in his voice, "Please, Emmy, please pick up when I call you, first time. Those seconds, minutes are a million years to me. And a whole lot of fucked-up shit goes through my mind in that time."

Straight away, I pull the phone from my jeans pocket and look down at the screen. Twenty-two missed calls. My heart drops.

"I'm so sorry. I fell asleep and didn't hear the phone."

I look up to Kayne and he's staring down at me. He stands and walks down the stairs.

I take a few steps back when he reaches the bottom and I notice the terror and sadness is gone, replaced by softness and the Kayne I fell in love with.

He reaches out and gently pushes my hair behind my ear. This time I don't flinch away. This time it feels somewhat natural and nice. Almost as though time turned back five years and I'm standing here in front of the man who just made love to me last night and we're saying goodbye to each other for the day, to head off to work.

"Still the most beautiful woman I've ever seen. You're breathtaking, Emmy. Not a day went by I didn't beg God to see your face, just one more time."

And just like that, memories invade my mind. Many men's hands, angry faces, hateful words. *Worthless, Used, Whore.*

I step back out of Kayne 's reach and his hand falls away and back to his side. His face slips back into sadness, but I can still see the determination in his eyes. Doesn't he realize my actions are the ones hurting him? Is he so blind by what he wants, he's missing the moments where I hurt him?

"I missed you, too," I admit.

Kayne 's eyes flare to life.

"But now it's time we both move on. Things have changed. You need to find someone else who you can have a life with, Kayne. "

Kayne shakes his head and his jaw ticks. "I already told you, Emmy. That's not happening. There is only ever going to be a me and you."

I growl. He's so frustrating. "Kayne, there is no us when I don't want you." I send that blow thinking it's going to affect him, but he doesn't react at all. Nothing in his strong-willed eyes changes.

"One day, one of us is going to move on, Kayne, whether you like it or not."

I need him to before my weak mind and body gives in to the man I love. Eventually, he will see how used and disgusting I am. Then I will be completely destroyed when he leaves me of his own free will. No one wants to exist in the dark when they can live in the light of day.

Kayne narrows his eyes at me.

"I'm warning you now, Emmy, if another guy comes onto the scene, I'm going to fuck him up. You try and push me away by using another man and I will be on your ass twenty-four fucking seven, making sure all the assholes in this town know you're mine. Whether you want to be or not."

With those words, he leaves the house, slamming the door behind him. Leaving me standing in the wake of his heavy words. That's something I would never do. Kayne will forever be the only man I will ever love or ever want to have in my life.

But I can't be selfish. I can do this. Endure more pain to save him. I'm hurting him, but I'm saving him from realizing the girl he loved so long ago is a ruined piece of flesh which can't be fixed or saved.

***

After Kayne left, I clean the house. There is dust everywhere. Everything I touch leaves my fingerprints behind. Jake wasn't kidding when he said Kayne was in Colombia for the past four years looking for me. It showed that he never returned to this house. I glance around and see how this home has been neglected and is now only a house.

Starting in the kitchen, I move systematically on to each room, one after the other. I leave the master bedroom until last. I spot the play, necklace and rose on the ground where I left them when I ran out to see who was at the front door. Picking them up, I clean off my dresser, place the rose back between the pages, and put them on top of the dresser where I will always be able to see them. I put the beautiful necklace around my neck; it fits perfectly.

When I finish cleaning, I'm hot and sweaty. I jump in the shower and wash away the sweat, as well as the day's ugliness. If only it was that easy to wash away the filthy parts of me. I long ago realized burning my skin with hot water doesn't wash the evil off.

After my shower, I cook up some chicken and vegetables I found in the freezer. I checked the dates to make sure they haven't been there for four years. But it appears Kayne stocked the fridge and cupboards before he moved out. Sitting at the big table on my own, I can't help but feel alone. I look around at the big house and the silence is deafening. If I try hard enough, I can hear the laughter of children who should have been, vibrating around this family home.

The laughter of my friends, from the collection, floats through my mind. I do miss them, sort of. Being near them always reminded me of where we were and why we were there. Today, I've found myself forgetting where I've been for the past five years, but only for mere seconds. However short those seconds may be, they are still moments of peace. A feeling of calmness my soul craves.

Chewing my chicken, I look into the kitchen

and a memory slams into my mind. One that has heat hitting me right between the legs. Which surprises me, I thought my body would reject these thoughts and emotions. But instead my thighs rub together and I'm yearning to have the same connection again.

Walking into the kitchen, I find Kayne cooking over the stove. He's shirtless with just a pair of board shorts on. His broad, smooth back is my second favorite body part on Kayne. I imagine scratching my nails down his back as he enters me and makes me feel the delicious pleasure of being full of him.

He turns around and sees me staring at him. His eyebrow quirks up in question and then quickly his stare turns heated as he realizes what I'm thinking about. He drops the tongs to the side and I watch as he turns the food off.

He walks around the bench, grinning at me.

"Something you need, Emmy?"

He wants me to ask, and soon I know he'll be making me beg for it.

"I want you to take me over the bench, from behind."

I'm not shy in asking for what I want. I used to be when we first moved out together. It took a lot of stuttering and embarrassing moments for me to tell

Kayne what I wanted. Kayne wouldn't give it to me otherwise; he loves it, no, gets off on it when I'm forward with him. With his constant praise of my body and his reassurance of his love for me, I moved past my insecurities a long time ago.

Kayne smiles big and licks his lips. "You got it, baby. Strip and bend over the bench."

I do as he says. The tingle between my legs growing with every piece of clothing I remove.

Kayne watches me, his heated, greedy stare running over my body. I watch as he clenches his fingers to stop himself from ripping the clothes from my body. It's happened before and I loved it, but Kayne loves the control that comes with sex and I don't care that I have to give up my power to him because I know his first priority is always me.

Naked, and wet between my legs, I walk over to the bench and bend my body over the top. I'm on my tippy toes, but the height is perfect. I grab hold of the other side of the bench and wait for the moment to come when I know Kayne will show me nothing less than euphoria.

I turn my head to the left and watch as he discards his shorts and he's left naked and beautiful. His cock is hard and his balls swollen. My hand itches to grab his balls and swirl them around in my hands.

Kayne comes up behind me and grasps my waist. His fingers are big and warm. He lifts my feet off the ground and spreads my legs. He pushes me further up on the bench until most of my body is lying flat on the counter. My pussy's on the edge and one leg is bent with Kayne holding the other straight out in the air. I can feel the cool air hit my sensitive folds and I moan at the thought of what will happen next.

Kayne bends, his front to my back. He drops kisses down my spine while his erection pushes into my wet folds. He circles his hips and pushes in with a small amount of pressure, before pulling back out. I whine, wanting him to go all the way inside me, hard.

I feel the rumble of a laugh through his front to my back. "Kayne," I breathe out, "no games this time, please. I want you inside me. Now."

"Okay, baby, no games this time, but I want you to go off twice, so first let me play a little."

And with those words, Kayne is down on the ground and his mouth is on me. Sucking, licking. Oh, God. I grip the edge of the bench tightly and push down. Kayne groans and cups my ass in his hands and pulls me deeper into his mouth. With shaking legs and sweat building behind my knees, my pussy contracts. A cry escapes my lips as my orgasm holds me prisoner for the sweetest seconds of my life.

My breathing heavy, the world comes back into focus. And then, I have my wish. Kayne thrusts into me from behind. I scream out in ecstasy. He drives into me hard, again and again. I love it. I moan loudly as my heart races and heat radiates up my legs.

"Fuck. I love being inside you, Emmy," Kayne growls between thrusts. "Tight. Wet. Fucking heaven, baby."

I gasp as my second orgasm slams into me. My whole body explodes like tiny fireworks all over my skin. Kayne thrusts come harder and faster, and then with a few grunts and a long groan, I know he just rode out his orgasm with mine.

I jump when I hear the cell ringing. I left it on the table so I could see it and hear it when Kayne called again. Hearing him scared today was both unusual and heart breaking. I don't ever want to do that to him again.

I examine the screen and see a picture of Kayne and me at a family barbecue. I'm sitting on his lap wrapped up in his arms and we're smiling happily up at the camera. God, what I would give to go back to that moment.

Realizing I've been distracted by the photo, I hastily try and answer. My fingers fumble trying to pick up the call. Finally, I'm able to answer by swiping upwards. I hear my name and I place the phone to my ear.

"Hi," I say quickly.

"Emmy." Kayne says my name and I can hear the anguish of our distance in his voice. I wrap my fingers around my glass orb necklace and close my eyes tightly. It's so painful to hear his desperation and feel my own at the same time.

There is silence for a long moment before Kayne speaks.

"For now, I won't push you for conversation. We'll work up to that. Thank you for picking up, baby. Until tomorrow. Night, Emmy."

Kayne doesn't hang up. I do it quickly. A frantic need to beg him to come over is on the tip of my tongue. I blink away one stray tear of loneliness and stare down at the device. I remember smart phones, but I haven't used one for five years and they're a hell of a lot thinner and longer.

I throw my food away, having lost my appetite after speaking to Kayne. I enter the bedroom and change into some pajamas. I look down at myself and see the white cotton shorts and white singlet. Something I use to wear to bed all the time, half a decade ago.

I walk over to the bed and just stare at it. So

many memories in this bed, wonderful, loving memories. I pull the covers back and slide under the comforter. It feels massive. I don't remember ever feeling that before. But back then, I wasn't sleeping alone. I wish I felt his presence with me. He was only here last night, yet I feel nothing, just a lot of lonely space around me.

Pulling the pillow from his side of the bed, I put it to my nose. It smells of shaving cream. I sigh. Kayne must have shaved last night. Contentment slowly flows through my body from having his familiar scent near me.

I hug the pillow to me and remember my thoughts from downstairs. The sex in the kitchen wasn't anything unusual for us. Any opportunity to have sex, Kayne and I would take it. Normal life was just that, normal. We laughed, worked, and visited our family. But sex when we joined, it connected us on another level. Looking into each other's eyes while we gave pleasure to the other, our eyes spoke for us, made promises we both knew the other would keep forever.

I want that life back. Anxiety floods me at having it all, but it being ripped away once again. But this time, it's taken away because of me, because he sees just how ugly my heart and soul has become.

Those moments when men stole pieces of me

are forever burned into my memory. I did give up fighting though. A small part of me hates myself because I gave up. Over time, I realized there was only so much fight in me. When I stopped fighting, the men would only use me to get off. It was easier to walk in and spread my legs. When I fought, they fought me back, harder. It excited them. So I stopped. I stopped giving them what they were coming to the parties for.

Donovan was the only man to hurt me when I didn't fight him in the first place. He never tired of trying to pull a reaction from me. He always came with renewed anger for me, something that always surprised me since I hadn't seen him for month's in-between. I prayed for the day he would go one-step too far and kill me. But he was obsessed with me, so he never let it go that far. Unfortunately.

My body freezes. Where is Donovan? Does he know I've been rescued? My breathing escalates and I look around the room wildly. Has he realized he will never see me again? My sight blurs and my head feels light. I remind myself. *Inhale, Exhale, Inhale, Exhale.* My heart calms and I begin to settle my panic. I hope he knows I'm gone. I hope it pulls apart his well-controlled world. He will have to find someone— I catch myself on that thought. *He will have to find someone else to take his anger out on. No!* I can't let someone else go through what I did. I can't let him do that. I need to stop him. For good this time. But how do I find him? There's only one person I know who might help me and have the connections to find Donovan.

I look at the clock and see its eleven pm. It's late, but I'm still going to try and call. I pick up my new cell phone and dial the number which had been repeated to me for years.

"If you ever escape and need help, call me on this number, 651-438-8604."

I place the phone to my ear and listen to the ringing tone. Finally, it clicks off and the person I'm searching for says a cautious, "Hello."

Chapter Seven

Kayne

I'm pacing up and down Dom's living room. I stop to glance around every few minutes, taking in the black furniture with a massive TV; it's a typical bachelor pad. I start pacing again. I'm coming out of my skin. Emmy's in our house. She's in our town. She was within touching distance today. Three times I've had to walk away from her since she's been back. Leaving her and our home today, nearly goddamn killed me. I felt my knees try to lock me in place while walking down the porch stairs, but I kept going. I kept walking away from my Emmy while my whole body begged me to stop and turn around.

I stop pacing and decide to try and get some sleep. Dom's away for three months on a job in Louisville. Dom is another friend who worked his ass off to find Emily. He's undercover at the moment, so I can't tell him I'm actually staying here, but I know he wouldn't care. We've all been friends since grade school. We aren't just friends; we're brothers. All of us, Jake, Dom, Nick and I. They had my back and put their lives on hold to help me find Emily. I'll never be able to repay them.

I wish one of them were here now to kick my ass out of this depressed state, but Jake's in Australia with Lily, Dom's undercover and Nick is doing actual work for our security company in Dallas.

I want my fucking life back. I want my Emmy back in my arms where she belongs. I know she's hurt. Jesus, hurt is a huge understatement. I shake my head. I can't go there, not yet. I can't think about how much she's been through or I'll never come out of my rage. I'd destroy this apartment and anyone who tried to calm me down.

I wonder if calling Emmy again would be okay. Probably not. I look at the clock. It's eleven pm. She's probably sleeping, in our bed. I growl and pull my hair roughly. Tomorrow. I can speak to her again tomorrow. *I wonder if she found the necklace I made for her. I hope she understood the message. We're meant to be, no matter what trials we go through.*

I take off my clothes and climb into bed commando. The way I've always slept. Emmy and I loved the feeling of skin on skin. We always went to bed naked. Whether we had sex or not, although it usually lead to sex. As soon as I would stroke her arm, she would shuffle her back and ass into me and then she'd grind against my cock, and that's all it took. My dick would grow hard and my hand would reach across her front to squeeze and caress her gorgeous tits until I heard her sweet moans, and that's all I could handle. Then I'd turn her over and claim her. Take what was mine. My girl.

I blow out a big breath and feel my dick grow hard. Fuck. It's been a long fucking time since I've felt the inside of Emmy's pussy. I've never strayed or been with anyone else in the last five years. I'd been with other girls before Emily, in high school, but never after Emmy, and I never will. As long as she still breathes the same air as me, she will be the only woman my cock craves.

What if Emmy never wants to be with me again? What will I do? How will I live? Seeing her, hearing about her but never being able to have her. All I've ever known my whole life is that Emmy is the other half of my heart. Even before we were together, she was mine. I was biding my time, waiting for her to grow up. Knowing she wanted me too.

Anger radiates through me. I grab the pillow and throw it across the room. *Fuck.* I want my fucking girl back.

I calm myself and flop back, lying on the bed. I will get her back. I'll do whatever I need to do to have my Emmy back where she belongs. I just need to be patient and strong. I can do that. I've done that for five years. What's another few months?

I hope that's all it will be.

Chapter Eight

One month being home

One month of therapist appointments and attempting to pretend to the outside world that I'm okay. I've been attending the appointments twice a week. My mom organized it for me. There was no hesitance from me when my mother asked me to go. Her glassy eyes and pleading face was all it took for me to tell her yes.

My mom took me the first time, but after that session, I felt as if someone had cut me open and taken out my carefully buried memories. I was raw and all I wanted to do was break down on my own. I needed space. I needed to be alone, to sit in a corner somewhere and take the assaults of the memories, take the slicing pain and put them back in their dark corners where they belonged. Dr. Zeek dug deep. I *hated* her. She was pulling apart my well-constructed world after only two hours. I felt weak all over again.

The look on my mother's face when I came out of the office was torture. Silent tears fell from her eyes as she drove me home. I wanted to scream. I wanted to tell her to leave me alone. Stop trying to help me because she was only hurting me. Bringing up these memories, seeing her pain, all of it was just too painful. I just wanted to pretend. I just wanted to be numb again.

I decided after that time, I would take myself from now on. If I had to go, I would go alone. To do that I needed my car and I needed to learn to drive again. My car was at my parents' house in their garage. My dad had been servicing it and running it every couple of months to make sure it would be ready for when I returned home.

A small ache hit my chest when I imagined him working on it all these years. Not knowing if I was dead or alive.

Learning to drive again was frustrating and exhilarating all at the same time. My dad took me out for my first test drive. Driving the car was fine, but learning the new road rules was frustrating.

The frustration didn't last long though. It was also liberating getting into a car and taking myself somewhere. I wasn't taken, dragged or driven. I was driving myself. I had control over where I wanted to go. It was freeing and for just a little while, all I thought about was the road in front of me. Not the past and not the pain.

My appointments with Dr. Zeek continued to be excruciating. Many times on my drive home, I imagined what it would be like to drive head on into a tree, off a bridge. Then it would all just end. The memories, the pain. Then my parents and Kayne could mourn me and move on. What they should have done five years ago. Forgotten about me. But I don't. I can't. Now and again, in the back of my mind in a small corner, a light flickers and I imagine a world where I smile. A life where my family looks at me proudly and I know it's because of everything I have overcome. I want that life so badly, but the light dims more every day. The other dark corners mock my ray of hope. They creep up on it like monsters in the night, cackling, knowing it's only a matter of time before they extinguish the light.

I do want Dr. Zeek to help me. I just don't think it's possible. I live in a world where harsh realities have scarred my soul. Where real hands have bruised my skin, where spoken words have seared my mind. What can Dr. Zeek do to undo all of that? My own mind turned against me and continues to torment me.

"Anything on your mind, Emily," Dr. Zeek asks. I look up from my fidgeting hands to Dr. Zeek and see her soft eyes watching me. I'm nervous.

Bile rises up my throat because I know how I will feel during this appointment.

"A bit," I reply. There's a lot, but I'm unsure of what she means.

"How are you settling in to your house? You've been there for three weeks now. Does it feel strange to live there alone?"

"I've lived on my own for the past five years, so no."

"But you had the women from the collection with you. So you weren't living alone," she states.

"We may have been in the same house but we were still all alone. We were all fighting our own demons."

I sit up straight in the chair and tap the floor with the toe end of my sandals. Whenever she gets close to talking about the collection women, I grow nervous. Those are memories I want locked up. I've thrown away the key and have no desire to go back to those memories. That is the one thing out of all of this mess I understand. Women were taken, abused and raped, and then they disappeared. I know what 'disappeared' means. They were killed. They didn't stop fighting; they didn't obey. So they were taken care of. I understand I couldn't have helped them. That was out of my control. My heart breaks for them and their families. But it is one thing, thank

God, I know doesn't sit heavy on my soul.

"Do you miss Kayne, Emily?" she asks and my breath stills. I promised myself I would tell the truth during these appointments.

"Yes," I whisper, "with all my heart. I miss him every day and every night."

"Have you told Kayne this?"

"No, and I won't. He wants us to be together, but he doesn't know what he's asking for. I won't let him close enough to see how worthless and used I am. I couldn't handle the rejection."

Dr. Zeek sits forward and narrows her eyes at me. "Do you know it usually takes me months or years to pull the self-loathing out of my clients? You just handed it to me. Why?"

I shrug. "What's to hide? I'm a whore. I've been with over thirty men. I've done unspeakable, disgusting acts. It's only a matter of time before everyone sees it."

"No, Emily. You were raped over thirty times. You were forced to do those things. You are not a whore."

"Does it matter if I was forced or not? They were still done to me."

Her words give me hope, yet they burn me because I know it's false. Anger bubbles inside me.

"I see a hundred different hands all over me. I

can still taste their semen in my mouth. I feel their fingers tightening around my throat when I fall asleep and when I wake. They burned the memory of feeling sore between my legs into my mind. They are everywhere. In my dreams, in my thoughts and in my memories. I don't even know if the man standing across the street from me is one of them because I can't remember all their fucking faces!" I end with a scream and stand breathing heavily.

"I understand your words, although I can never understand your feelings as I've never lived what you have lived, Emily. What you are feeling is valid and warranted, but if you don't try to move past what you think you have become, those thoughts and those memories are going to have you frozen in time. There is a way to lessen the effect they have on you. You need to open yourself up to the possibility that you are more than what they said you are."

"How?" I whisper to the window.

"You need to take back your power. Stop giving it to the demons in your mind. You keep saying what you don't deserve. Start thinking about what you do deserve. Stop punishing yourself for the things that were out of your control. You never wanted them. Don't let them take any more than they already have, Emily."

Each time I leave her office, I race home and sit in the same corner in the spare room. Here, I grasp a tight hold of my glass rose necklace and cower in the corner while my mind wages war with itself. The old words with the new. Doubts the swords and hope the shields. A little while ago, I began scratching my arms with my nails. When it became too much, I needed to distract myself and think about something else. The only thing strong enough to do that was physical pain, so I scratched my arms with my nails. I don't bleed often, but the last time I did, and I scared myself, though it worked. I distracted myself and I was able to move past the tormented moment.

Kayne called me every day for the first week, sometimes twice a day. I picked up every time. He would ask about my day and if I needed anything. The same questions all the time. Sometimes there was just silence for long moments. My heart would pound heavily and my palms would sweat. The strength to hold back telling him how much I loved him was taking its toll on me. I would rush to say goodbye before my voice became strangled.

After that week, he started coming over, either in the mornings or in the afternoons. He would bring me some breakfast or tells me he was just checking the mailbox. I'd cling to these moments. I'd look forward to them as much as I dread them, but I realized this was what Kayne 's life had become. I have pulled this wonderful man down with me to the depths of misery where he also counts on these small occasions. These moments are becoming our lives, our reasons for living. That's not what I want for Kayne. I need him to move on.

***

Forty days of being home and today was the worst. I cut my skin open with a razor. The memories were too much. I had to release the pain and the evil filling my veins.

I'm fucked up, but I know enough that what I'm doing isn't healthy and I'm not getting better; I'm getting worse. The nightmares through the night slammed into me like a cement wall. I needed something to overtake my thoughts, and at the time, I felt as if my own blood was the enemy and I needed to expel its toxic vileness from my body.

My heart shattered as I watched the blood spill down my thigh and I realized I am this weak, pathetic excuse of a woman.

I feel worthless. I'm learning I'm not, but I *feel* that way. I want it to stop, but I just *can't*.

Chapter Nine

Two months of being home

Not much has changed except I'm sick of hiding away in the house. Today, I have the urge to venture out. I head for the museum. I don't think I'm at risk of seeing Kayne, my family or anyone I may know at a museum in the middle of the day on a Thursday. I have this sudden urge to see beautiful pictures. For the last five years, all that was in front of me was ugliness.

I dress in denim shorts and a black, capped-sleeve top. I hop in my silver Mazda3 and start her up. The vibration of the engine sends a jolt to my heart. The ability to go anywhere on my own is still new to me. Excitement courses through my veins.

It doesn't take long before I'm at The Minneapolis Institute of Arts. Walking through the long hallways, examining the artwork on the walls, I come to a picture where men are standing behind a barbed wire fence in black and white striped trousers and jackets. I read the title of the picture.

Holocaust. The Living Dead at Buchenwald, 1945.

Their faces tell of hope lost. Families ruined. Souls damaged beyond repair. They've been beaten down and given no light at the end of the tunnel. The picture causes my heart to ache so I move on.

The next picture is of four elderly men, their ages I'm guessing would be somewhere in the eighties or nineties. Each has an arm around the next and all of them with smiles on their faces. I read the statement at the bottom.

Holocaust Survivors, 2005.

I read the names from left to right. I look up to their picture and study each smile. Each man's grin is unique and tells of a life now filled with happiness.

A small piece of warmth hits my chest. They survived Hell. They actually lived in Hell with thousands of evil men. Could I one day be like them? Smiling and happy. A survivor, actually surviving happily?

I'm unsure how long I stand there staring at the picture of the four happy elderly men, but at some point it hits me. If I saw these men out in the streets, I would never know what they had been through. I look around the hallway and see three other people in a group regarding pictures, talking to each other and smiling. What if these people had been through horrors themselves? Yet they are smiling, happy. How do they do that? Move to the place that allows them to smile again?

I want to buy a camera. I want to capture those smiles on people's faces. I want to find the answer. People everywhere struggle through hard times. Grief, heartache, and like me, rape. They still carry on; they still smile. I want to capture those moments and fill my life with them. I want to learn how they do that, how they survive and do it with a smile on their face.

***

I'm at home fiddling with my new camera I just bought, a Canon 600D. Kayne gave me a bankcard a few weeks ago; he said it was our joint account. He told me to use it. I vowed not to. I didn't want to spend his hard-earned money, but this was important. I need this camera.

The front door handle rattles and I know its Kayne unlocking it. It's that time of the day for him to come over and say he's checking the mail, but he comes inside and checks the fridge and stares at me instead.

The door opens and I watch the most beautiful man walk through. His blue, soft eyes look from the handle to mine. I'm flashed to an impossible future where this could have been Kayne coming home from work. *"Daddy's home, yay!" Our two beautiful children race each other down the stairs to cuddle their father. Kayne scoops them up into his arms and gives them a kiss each on their cheeks. Then comes to me, his wife and gives me a heart stopping, passionate kiss because he missed me so much in the eight hours he's been gone for.*

"Emmy, you okay?"

I'm shaken from my fantasy. I nod quickly and go back to reading the instructions on my camera.

"What's that, Emmy?" Kayne asks, pointing to the camera.

"I went to the museum today and decided I wanted to buy a camera. I want to take pictures." I glance at Kayne to view his reaction.

"Pictures of what, baby?"

I cringe when he uses the endearment. It sends false hope to my heart and I'm left with the wild beating inside my chest. He notices, he always does, but he keeps calling me it.

"I want to take pictures of people." I see the confusion on Kayne 's face but I just shrug. I'm not sure how to explain to him why I want the camera.

"Um, that's good, Emmy, and you left the house today. Maybe next time you can let me know when you go and I can come with you."

I sigh. He knows I want him to leave me alone, but he doesn't and he won't. I shrug once again and go back to studying my new camera. Out of the corner of my eye, I watch Kayne observe me for a minute and then he moves to the fridge.

"Emmy, you're low on food. I told you to tell me when you needed something."

I take in the contents of the fridge. Hmm, I do need food. This is just another reason why Kayne feels he needs to look after me. Damn, I need to start taking care of myself so he doesn't have to check up on me. I stand from the table.

"I'll head to the store now."

"I'll go with you. We can take my car," is Kayne 's reply as I grab my car keys.

"No, I can take myself and shop on my own. I'm sure you have other things to do, Kayne."

"Yes, I do Emmy. I have a fuckload of shit I *need* to do. But what I *want* to do is take you to the store and spend some time with you."

I sigh once more and drop my car keys to the table knowing I'm not going to win this conversation. I head for the front door and then I pivot, race back into the dining room, and grab my new camera.

We head out to Kayne 's black SUV and drive in silence to the grocery store, while I snap pictures of people we pass.

We arrive at the supermarket and grab a cart. Kayne pushes while I snap some more pictures. I spot a store attendant, who is smiling brightly and saying hello to everyone who passes her as we enter the store. She looks at me strangely after I take the picture. I step closer to Kayne and look around the store as if I never took the picture. It never crossed my mind what people would think if they knew I was taking pictures of them.

I hear a chuckle, look to Kayne and see him grinning at me.

"So you brought a camera to take pictures of grocery store attendants?"

"No, yes. I brought the camera to take pictures of everyone. Beautiful people," I reply.

"And chicks in ugly, yellow and blue uniforms are beautiful to you?" he asks, surprised.

"Every person who can smile in this world is beautiful and lucky," I state, picking up some carrots and putting them in the cart.

When I pick up a bag of potatoes and look for the cart, I see Kayne hasn't moved on with me. He's staring at me with intensity. A stare that expresses his understanding and sadness for me. I glance away and try to busy myself to ignore the need to have his arms wrapped around my body so he can fix the broken I have inside me.

Kayne and I move around the supermarket silently. Before I was taken, we would fight over who was pushing the cart. We would laugh, touch, and kiss our way through the food shopping.

"Kayne, I can push a cart," I say as he tries to nudge me to the right to be in front of the handlebars.

"I know, baby, but it's full. It's got to be heavy. Just give it to me." I choose to ignore him and push the mildly heavy cart.

"Emmy, let me push the cart," Kayne says these words in a low tone. One I'm sure he reckons will make me think he means business. I keep my head straight and continue to ignore the huge man trying to push me out the way.

"You know what will happen next, baby," he states.

I turn and glare at him. I'm wondering if he's talking about spanking me later or tickling me right now. I tend to snort when I laugh. It's quite embarrassing. If Kayne is threatening that right now, in this grocery store, which is full of people, then he is in so much trouble.

Kayne's grin grows wider at my glare. "I'm going to enjoy spanking your ass later. But don't think I won't tickle you for the cart, right now."

I stop dead in my tracks and Kayne takes his hand from the cart and narrows his eyes on me.

"You wouldn't dare." I know I'm initiating the dare with those words, but there's no way he's going to do this, over a cart!

"I can see you having to pull against your body when you stop to pick something. That means the cart is too fucking heavy for you, Emmy. You're my girl. I'm walking right next to you. That shit is not cool if I just let you keep deep breathing like you ran a marathon just to stop the fucking cart. So yes, I will tickle you for the cart. Win-win for me. I love your snorts. They make me fucking hard."

I roll my eyes at his over-reaction of me stopping the cart. I look around and assess how many people are around us and who would hear me. As I'm looking around, I feel his hand under my arm and I scream. In one jump, I let go of the cart and Kayne has it firmly in his grasp.

Damn him. "Are you happy? You have the precious cart now." I stomp off away from him and Kayne laughs out loud.

I'm standing, looking over the spreads when I feel his arm wind around my waist and his lips press on my neck. I fight the urge to sink into his body. I last about three seconds when he whispers, "I'm just saving your energy for later, baby. I'm going to spank your ass and tickle you breathless."

Heat explodes down below and my body betrays me as I sink into Kayne 's chest.

I find myself holding my rose glass necklace. I give it a quick squeeze before I decide to distract myself from the memories by snapping a few more pictures of people shopping. Couples and families together. All of them smiling and happy. I wonder about what adversaries they've fought through and are now smiling.

We finish buying groceries and Kayne drives us back to the house. We put the food away together in more awkward silence. Sometimes Kayne leaves with a quiet goodbye, other times he starts up with us getting back together. I sense today is one of those days he wants to talk again and it's making me jittery. It kills me to keep reliving rejecting him.

"Emmy—" Kayne starts, but I cut him off.

"No, please, Kayne. Please don't go there. I've told you my answer a hundred times and it hasn't changed."

Kayne 's face falls, just like it does every time.

"How many times do I have to tell you, I'm not the Emily you fell in love with."

"Then show me the new Emily. I will love her too. Whatever mask you wear, I will love them all," Kayne states firmly.

My mouth drops open and my eyes widen. *When will he give up!*

Kayne must see the question on my face because he answers it for me.

"I'm never giving up, Emmy. Don't think I can't read you like a book. I know what you're doing. Pushing me away because you think for some fucking reason you're saving me. But you aren't. Being away from you is killing me. But that's okay. I understand why, but I'm not going anywhere. I'm staying right here. Every goddamn day I will be here reminding you of how much I love you. I'm. Never. Giving. Up. I know you love me, Emmy. It's in your eyes every time you watch me step into this house and every time you hold your necklace."

I drop my hand from my necklace not even realizing I'm holding it for strength to endure this conversation. My eyes sting and I will them not to cry. I have no idea what to say, how to deter him. I decide to go with the truth. I have no idea what else to do.

I throw up hands up in the air. "I'm not good enough for you anymore. I can't even smile, let alone ever laugh again. Feeling happy is a fucking miracle for me. Do you want that for your future? To have some depressed woman by your side forever. I'm not the fun, happy, free-spirited

Emily you fell in love with. You *have* to start understanding so you can move on."

"Never. I glimpse her every time I walk into this house and you look at me like you used too. I see her, right now, trying to protect me, the man you love. Whatever is going through your head about not being good enough or trying to give me a better future, it's wrong, Emmy. I can see it's going to take more time than I thought for that to sink in and for you to realize I'm not going anywhere, no matter what words you sling my way. I was here twelve years ago. I'm here now, and I will be here fighting for you until the day I die."

Kayne takes two steps and kisses my temple. I'm frozen from his determined words and now I'm stone still from his touch.

"I'll see you tomorrow, Emmy," Kayne says softly and then walks out of the house.

I'm left staring at the counter in the kitchen trying to remember if he was always this stubborn. *Yes, yes, he was.*

Chapter Ten

Kayne

It's Saturday and I'm pulling into Emmy and Jakes parents' house for a barbecue. Jake and Lily are heading back to Australia this week, so Ken and Barb are having a get together before they leave. Jake takes Lily back every few months. Usually, they only stay for about a week, but each time they leave, they hope to stay for at least a month. I know Lily struggles to be at her old home for too long. I can't blame her. The memories must be torture.

I hop out of my truck and I look around and find exactly what I'm searching for. Emmy's car. She's here.

I walk into the house and my heart stops. I lock my knees to stop myself from falling to the ground. A soft, musical, feminine laugh, one I've only heard in my dreams for the past five years rings through my body. I lean on the wall and lower my head, clenching my eyes closed. My Emily. My Emmy's carefree, beautiful laughter. My mind takes me on a roller coaster ride, through my memories of every time she's smiled up at me, like I'm everything in the world to her. My eyes sting and my body shakes. I need to get a hold of myself.

"Kayne?"

My head whips up at hearing her gorgeous sweet voice say my name. Her hand rests on my shoulder. While her other arm cradles a baby, her eyes narrow on me with an inquisitive look. I quickly stand straight and regret it instantly as her hand falls off my shoulder.

"Is everything okay?" she asks me.

I want to say no, everything is not okay because I still sleep alone at night, dreaming of how good she feels, dreaming of pulling her into my body and fighting off all her demons for her.

Emmy looks at me with the same blank face, but her eyes say everything. Every time they ghost over my features, want and need flash in her eyes, and I'm reminded me why I'm doing this, why I'm fighting for us all on my own. Emmy may not realize it, but she's fighting for herself and I can see it's taking all her strength. I have enough for both of us. I just wish she would realize it and let me in.

The baby in her arms starts crying and Emmy instantly looks to the child and starts cooing. *Fuck.*

That's what I was hearing. Her cooing a baby, not laughing. Not that it really matters; it's one-step forward. She's holding a child and comforting it. The Emmy from a few months ago would have denied holding the child at all.

"It's okay, Jacob. Mommy's getting you a bottle. Hang in there, little guy."

The baby instantly stops crying and tries to grab for Emmy's face. I understand, buddy; she's beautiful. I've stopped what I'm doing plenty of times just to stare at her.

"This is Carly's son," she states.

Carly is a friend of Emmy's from high school and college. She became close to Ken and Barb while Emmy was missing. She's married and has a daughter, Sophia, who is three and I had heard she had another baby recently.

I nod and give my girl a kiss on the temple. She doesn't resist or tense up. It's been two weeks since our grocery adventure. Emmy has tried very hard to ignore me and our conversations, except our phone calls. She knows how important they are to me. I need those at the end of the day as much as I require air. I have to know she's safe and well before I can sleep.

I keep reminding her I'm not going anywhere. I turn up at our house wanted or not. And now, I kiss her temple when I leave. It's a promise, a promise I'm here and I will be back the next day.

I stare at Emmy and see her watching the baby. He holds her pinkie tightly with his little fist. Emmy's eyes are sparkling. It's the happiest I've seen her since she came home.

"Kayne, hi!" I hear Carly say from behind me.

Emily and I both turn and spot Carly holding a baby's bottle.

"Hey, Carly, beautiful baby boy. Congratulations," I reply.

"Thanks, Kayne, Em is helping me feed him. He's very grumpy and Em was the only one he would stop crying with."

I turn to Emmy. "It's her face. Her beauty would stop any male in his tracks."

Emily's head whips up and her eyes pierce into mine. I can see everything she's thinking. Why do I keep being nice? Saying sweet things about her when she's constantly rejecting me? But I see my girl every day. I see the hurt she inflicts on herself when she rejects me. She's lost and trying to find her way. However, my girl is a fighter. I know she will find her way through this darkness and I won't let her walk this road alone. Emily has never been as real to me as she has been in the last few months. Her whole world right now is about trying to protect me, give me the best life I could possibly have. If that isn't love, I don't know what is. I'm going to fill Emmy's life with more happy memories than bad. We are going to bury the nightmares under dreams so it hurts less and less every day. I just need her to start trusting me. To start trusting it's her and only her forever.

I observe Emmy starting to retreat, her face closes down, and her eyes narrow. She's calling up all her strength to reject me again. I decide to give her a reprieve this time.

"Is Phillip here?" I ask Carly.

"Yeah, he's out back with Sophia and everyone else."

I nod and walk past a stunned Emily, through the kitchen and out the back to the covered pergola area.

First thing I see is Jake wrapped around Lily. Her giggles filter through the crowd and most people stop to look and listen. Watching them together gives me hope. What they went through, it's enough to break anyone, but they fought through it together and came out stronger. I know that will be Emmy and me. It has to be. I won't accept anything else.

As I watch my best friend with the love of his life, I almost miss the flash of brown that whips past the side of the house. I focus and realize its Emmy; she has her camera. She's kneeling on the lawn in the corner, camera lens extended and pointed at Jake and Lily.

Fuck, that breaks my heart.

Every day I walk into our house, there are more pictures of strangers. Emmy prints them out and has them sitting on the dining room table. When I asked her why she printed out pictures of strangers and have them in our house, her reply was, "They're beautiful. They smile even though there is evil in the world, and at one point, it has or could touch them, but still they smile." Broke my heart because when she said that and then looked up at me, her emotions were all over her face. She longed to know how they did it, how they can still smile and be happy. I can see how desperate she is to learn the secret. I want to hand it to her, on a silver fucking tray every day. If only she would let me.

***

Emily

Click. Click. Click. Click.

Looking through my lens, I stare at her smile. It looks like a puzzle on her lips that I need to figure out so I can do it too. Lily smiles effortlessly with Jake. She laughs. How? She lost everything. How does she smile at all?

I look around the yard through my lens.

Click. Click. Click. Click.

Everyone's laughing, smiling. Happy.

My pulse is beating quickly and my heart is pounding. I drop the camera to my chest and it hangs from my lanyard. I try to calm my breathing. I want what they have. Please, I need this pain to stop. I claw at my skin, ripping at my skin. Beads of blood come to the surface and drip down my arm. See I bleed like them. I'm human. Why can I not be happy like them? Why can I not move on like they have? At some point in their lives, they have hurt. Why can they move on and I can't?

I pick up my camera and furiously start taking more pictures. My finger gradually slows with tiredness. When I suddenly stop, my lens falls on Kayne. He's staring at me. His face intense, a frown in place. The only other person at this barbecue who isn't smiling. That's my fault. I have nightmares in my mind, but I'm Kayne 's. Deep down, I knew he would never let me go. I know how deep our love runs. Now I feel like I'm in a race to fix myself so I can make him happy too. *I'm so sorry God stuck you with me, Kayne.*

I stand and walk into the house. I watch Kayne from the corner of my eye, making sure he doesn't follow. I need to wash the blood away from my arm and I don't want him seeing what I've done to myself. It's nothing like the cuts on my thighs. But even Kayne seeing me just scratch myself, makes me nervous.

I close the bathroom door and rest my camera on the counter. I begin cleaning the blood off until all that is left are tiny, red swollen lines up my arms. I glance from my arm to my reflection in the mirror. My necklace catches my eyes. I wish at that moment I lived in a world with witches and fairies. Some type of fantasy creature which could send me back in time to when I had it all. I'd ask to go back and re-live my night with Kayne over and over again.

I jump when I hear the door open and then relax when I see its Lily. She looks into the room, spots me and then looks behind her, decides to come in and shuts the door.

I quickly pull my arm behind my back and say, "Hey, do you need to use the bathroom?"

I move to grab my camera, but Lily reaches out and grabs my hand. She flips it over and sees the red marks. Her eyes grow soft and she says gently, "Em, talk to me please."

I shake my head. "I'm okay—" I stop and realize what I should be asking her. "I want to ask you something; however, I don't want to sound rude or uncaring."

"Em, we're past this. You can ask me anything. I promise I won't take offense."

"How are you happy? I can't feel it, joy, about anything. I want to. But I just feel sad all the time."

What I don't say is I feel dirty, worthless, and pathetic. I don't want those words to leave my lips again. Each time they have, I felt like I gave them more power over me.

I watch as Lily's eyes go glassy at my question and statement.

"Oh, Em," Lily breathes out. "I'm happy and sad. I take each moment as it comes. I have my bad days. Sometimes, I need help from Jake to remind me why I'm still living and why I keep going. Your brother is closing the hole more and more every day with his love and support. If you let Kayne in, he can do the same for you."

I shake my head. "What if he gets too close and realizes how damaged I am, realizes I'm not good enough for him."

"Em, you have been through hell and back, but you are not damaged. And you *are* good enough for Kayne, for any man who you wanted to be with. As hard as it sounds, you need to let go of the past and embrace your future. It's up to you where your life will go from here. Right now, you're making decisions based on your fears. No good can come from that. I choose to see the good in the world instead of the bad which was forced onto me. And with the help of your brother seeing the good is easy, the days, weeks and months have gotten easier."

"But all I do is hurt Kayne. I'm afraid I'll only be dragging him down into this nightmare with me."

"He loves you, Emily. As long as you are frozen in this nightmare, he will be too. Love means you are never alone, whether you want to be or not," Lily says softly.

"I know," I rush out to say. "I'm trying, I am, but I just can't cross that fucking invisible line into happy land with everyone else," I say frustrated, staring into her eyes, begging her to help me.

Lily grasps my hands and squeezes tightly.

"That's because you're trying to cross it alone. You can't cross it until you realize you need help and that you are worth helping."

My stomach drops as I feel the line turn into a huge chasm that may possibly swallow me whole.

Chapter Eleven

I'm at home just getting out of the shower and dressing in my pajamas. Today was hard. The talk with Lily didn't give me any answers, only more questions. I understand the words she said, *just let Kayne in*. Let someone who loves me in, to help support me, but it's not that simple. If I let in the one man who loves me and he finds out what happened to me, what I took part in; I could lose him and not just be robbed of seeing him. Lose his love for me, his idea of who he thinks I am. It's all that's left of me. Thoughts from people who used to know me. If I don't have those anymore, then I really am lost to the darkness. If they find out who I have become, what's stopping the nightmare from taking me completely?

And if he accepts me? What life can I give him? Dark thoughts and cowering in a corner crying because I can't handle my past. Hiding in a bathroom cutting my skin just to give myself some moments of peace. Sooner or later he's going to have enough. My body sags. I'm so lost.

I head downstairs and print out the pictures I took at the barbecue. The dining room is now covered in pictures of strangers and now family members smiling and laughing. Living. I hear my cell ding and I look down and see it's a message.

Emailed you pictures.

My body stills. Pictures of *him*. Am I ready to see him again? It's been almost three months, the same amount of time it's been for the last year. Right around this time, I would have to be ready for a party. To be paraded in front of dozens of men and sold for the night. And for the past three years, he has been the highest bidder; he always won.

I race into the living room and pull the laptop out from under the coffee table. Kayne and I never used it much. Just for paying bills and emails from friends. I click onto the internet and I'm relieved to see we still have WI-FI for the house. I didn't think to check when I gave out my email address in the phone conversation.

I open up the email account I created and find an email there with the subject.

I found him.

I click on it and find pictures of the man who

made my life hell. One of the men, who created this Emily, the weak Emily. The one man who kept coming back to torture me. Donovan. He's dressed in another expensive suit. He's talking to a man. They are both wearing sunglasses and are in what looks like a park. I read the message in the email.

I'm in Mexico City. The man he's with is Marco's brother, Michael O'Connor. He's been asking questions about what happened to his brother and there are rumors he's set to start off where Marco's empire died.

From my Intel, I've found out Donovan has arranged this meeting with Michael in hopes of finding you.

Chills run through my body. Starting the collection again? *No!* And Donovan wants to find me, why? Would he try to kidnap me? *Of course he would; he's a psychopath.* I need to prepare. I need to catch him before he can find me, here with my family and with Kayne. I won't let him hurt them.

I reply to the email.

I need you to keep him in your sights. I need to know where he is at all times. When I figure out what my plans are, I will contact you through this email.

I grab a pen and paper and write list of things

I'm going to need.

Money, passport, ropes, zip ties, gag, knives, gun.

I see an email appear out of the corner of my eye.

Consider it done. Will I be seeing you soon?

I reply.

As soon as I can get out of Hastings, I will be there.

A memory of Donovan on top of me, holding me down, squeezing my throat so tight my vision blurs.

"That's right, Emily, you stupid whore, fucking pass out on me. You can't fucking hack it, can you! Worthless piece of shit," he screams at me as my world turns black. I wake feeling sore between my legs and my head pounding, alone in the room.

I come out of my memory, scratching over the cuts on my thighs. I need to take it out. I need to remove the poison from me, now. I race up the stairs, two at a time. I slam open the top draw where I know the shavers are. I snap the plastic off from around the razor until all I'm holding is the blade between my fingers.

I take a seat on the toilet lid. My hand shakes as I lift my cotton shorts, high up my thigh. I see three lines of cuts, all in a row. If anyone ever saw them,

I would say they are cat scratches.

I push the razor to the first line and feel a small sting, my heart starts racing and then I pull the blade through my skin toward me about three centimeters and release the blade from my thigh.

I exhale heavily as I feel the release run through my body. It wipes out the memory of his face. The memory of anything. My body relaxes and I lie back on the toilet and rest my head on the wall. My eyes close and my mind clears. *Peace.*

I come out of my daze to a lone, warm tear hitting my lips. Shame slams into me and I look down and see red smearing the cut. The brightest color in my world yet its mere existence tells me how weak I am.

I grab for the toilet paper and rip off a few sheets. I press down hard on the cut wishing it would magically disappear. Wishing it never happened. Bile rises in my throat and sweat coats my forehead. I'm so disappointed in myself. Why do I cut? I'm not completely sure. To have proof of my hurt? To match the ugliness I know is inside of me? I promise myself this will never happen again. I say it over and over again in my head. Whispers echo through my mind that I'm lying to myself, but I push them aside.

I flush the toilet paper and put a Band-Aid over

my swollen cut. I'm heading back downstairs when I hear my cell ringing. I stop and look around. It's probably around eight pm, which means its Kayne.

I race down the stairs to my phone, which is sitting on the dining room table.

"Hello." My voice is soft with a slight shake to it.

"Hey, Emmy." At hearing Kayne's voice my chest constricts and tears start falling. I want him here. I want Kayne to hold me and tell me everything is going to be okay. The strength I need for these conversations has already depleted. I need to make this quick or I'm going to fall apart on the phone to him.

"Kayne, I'm tired can we talk tomorrow, please." My voice starts out strong but by the end it's shaky. I berate myself for not being strong.

"Emmy, is everything okay?" I can hear Kayne moving around while he's on the phone.

"Yes, yes. It's just..." I shake my head trying to think of what to say. But what can I say? If I told Kayne I have pictures and know the whereabouts' for a man who raped me, he would go ballistic. He would go after him, and that's the last thing I want. I don't want the dark part of my life anywhere near Kayne. If anyone is going to deal with Donovan, it will be me.

"Emmy, what the fuck is going on? You sound scared. I'm coming over."

"No, Kayne, really—" That's all I get out before he hangs up. Damn it.

My pulse speeds up and I start panicking. I put the phone down and slam the laptop closed. I race into the living room and put it back under the coffee table. I look around wildly and realize I'm being silly. Kayne 's not going to find out I'm tracking Donovan and he's not going to walk through the door in the next two seconds. I slump down on the couch and try to regain some sanity.

I head toward the kitchen to heat up some leftovers from the barbecue my mom made me bring home. As the microwave dings at eight minutes, I hear the front door unlocking and Kayne 's booming voice through the house.

"Emily!"

"In the kitchen!" I pull my plate out of the microwave and turn as Kayne walks into the kitchen.

"If you hadn't hung up on me, I was going to tell you I'm fine, Kayne," I state.

I walk into the dining room with my plate and move some pictures over. I sit and start eating my rissole and potato salad.

"Bullshit, Emily, I know you better than that

and you know I do. Something happened. What was it?" he asks sternly.

Damn, I do know that. I should never have picked up his phone call, but I needed to hear his voice. I needed to remember where I am and that I'm safe. I decide to lie. I do not want Kayne finding out I'm looking for my abuser.

"I had a bad memory, that's all," I state softly.

Kayne takes the seat next to me. He sighs and drops his head. God, my heart hurts for him. I know how badly he wants to help me. He just can't. Nobody can.

Kayne sits up and leans back in his chair, his hands clasped together on the table.

"I'm staying the night," he states. My eyes go wide and my mouth drops open. *No!*

"No, you're not, Kayne. "

"Why not, Emmy? You said you had a bad memory. I can't go back to Dom's and sit around wondering if you're going to have another and no one is here for you. Or fuck, how many moments have you had like that already. No fucking way, I'm here tonight. I'll sleep on the couch."

Kayne moves away from the table.

"I'm taking a shower and getting ready for bed. Luckily, most of my clothes are already here," he says and smirks at me before disappearing up the stairs.

Kayne leaves me sitting at the table with my untouched food. I stare into thin air realizing I'll be spending the night with Kayne. Well, not with him, but in the same house. It's been over five years. *God.* I can't handle this. My body heats up just seeing him. This is going to be torture. I smack my forehead on the table and repeat quietly, "I can do this. I can do this."

A few minutes later, my eyes shift to the bottom of the staircase as I hear Kayne 's loud footsteps come down the stairs. Sweat builds on my neck and I lick my lips as Kayne walks to me in just a towel. I swallow and it goes down hard.

"I left my toothbrush in the car." He grins and walks out the front door. A minute later, he's back inside, the door closing, and locking. He turns and winks at me and then he's gone back up the stairs again. Jesus, I think I just stared at him the whole time. *Toothbrush in his car?* Why would his toothbrush be in the— that man! He knew he was going to stay all along.

I decide to let it go. He's here. He's staying and it's not going to change by me telling him I know he planned it. *I want him here.* No, I can't think like that; he can't get too close.

Chapter Twelve

I finish my dinner and grab two blankets for Kayne. As I enter our bedroom to retrieve him a pillow, I notice the shower is running in the ensuite. He's using the ensuite shower. Goddamn it. Now when I go in there, it's going to smell like him. I snatch up his pillow and stomp out of the room. I swear he chuckles as I leave the room.

I'm pulling the sofa bed out of the couch, unsuccessfully; this bed is a bitch to pull out, and it appears it hasn't gotten any better in the last five years. I'm pulling when I see Kayne walking down the stairs in a pair of long, black cotton pants and nothing else. Goddamn him! I put all my anger into pulling the sofa out, but the bed pops right out and sends me flying backward. I hit the floor and then feel an arm behind my back, stopping me from hitting the solid wood TV unit. A grunt reverberates in my ear at the same time I see one of Kayne's arms reach up and catch the TV before it falls on my head.

After I realize what's happened, I look to my right and observe Kayne 's face cringing in pain. I squashed his arm between the TV unit and me. I jump up with a squeal.

"Oh, my God, are you okay?"

Kayne pulls his arm to his front and holds it as if it's broken. "Yeah, baby, I'm okay, but you need to be more careful. You could have seriously hurt yourself doing that. That bed has a fucking huge spring to it when it's pulled out. Don't you remember?"

I search my memories and yes, I do remember. I was just too focused on Kayne 's naked chest and my anger to remember it at the time.

I reach out my arm and say, "Show me your arm, Superman. You should never have done that."

"Whatever, of course I would do that and I would do it every fucking time. But from now on, you let me pop the bed out, okay?" Kayne asserts the question firmly.

"Fine," I say with a stubborn tone. "Now, show me your arm, Kayne," I state with narrowed eyes to show him I mean business.

He sighs and turns his arm over. I hiss at finding a bruise already forming and he has a swollen welt that's bleeding.

"I'll just go grab the first aid kit," I mutter to myself as I turn to walk to the kitchen.

I pull open the cupboards under the sink. There sits our green first aid kit. There are spider webs attached to it and the plumbing. I pull it out and run a tea towel over it. I open it up, pull out the antiseptic wipes and the large square Band-Aids.

I walk back into the living room and find Kayne sitting on the sofa bed spreading out the sheets.

"Here, some antiseptic to clean it and Band-Aids if you want them." I place them on the coffee table and stand back, unsure what to do. Five years ago, I would have cleaned his cut myself and then followed that up with some thank-you sex. I look around the room nervous.

"What, you aren't going to clean it for me, Emmy?" Kayne says with a smirk.

I shake my head at his playful nature and feel my face soften as I admire his smile.

"You're a big boy, Kayne. You've looked after yourself for the last five years. I'm sure you can handle a small cut."

Instantly, my heart dies at my words when I realize what's passed my lips.

Kayne 's smile dies a quick death and I feel horrible.

"Shit, I'm so sorry. I shouldn't have said that."

Kayne doesn't acknowledge my apology. Roughly, he begins to clean his cut. Then he stands, stares at me with a hard look, and walks into the kitchen. I'm guessing to throw away the antiseptic wipe or maybe cool off.

I slowly walk to the staircase unsure how to fix what my stupid big mouth just said. I feel a warm hand on my elbow as I take the first step. I turn and see Kayne 's beautiful face.

"Please, don't go to bed yet, Emmy. Let's talk. Please," he pleads.

His warm, familiar hand on my elbow is like stepping out into the sunshine for the first time in a long while of being locked up inside a dark room. It's both agonizing and blissful at the same time. The warmth spreads up my arms and threatens to crack my whole chest wide open and bring down my façade. I nod slowly, unsure if I can trust my voice.

Kayne moves his hand away as I walk back to the living room and immediately my body begs me to recapture his touch.

Kayne takes a seat on the sofa bed and I sit on the single sofa.

"What do you want to talk about?" I ask.

"You. I want to know how you're doing, Emmy."

I sigh, "I'm still struggling, but I'm always going to struggle, Kayne. That's why you need to move on. I don't want this life for you. This gloomy, miserable black world I live in. There's no color, no smiles and no happiness in store for me. It kills me to think this could be your future, Kayne, when you deserve so much more."

"I deserve more? Emmy, you deserve just as much as anybody else. And the gloomy, miserable black world you live in can become color. You can be happy again. You just need to let me help you. We can make enough good memories to fade out the bad. You just have to let us *try,* baby. You're not the only person who went through hell while you were gone, Emmy. My world was black before I found you. Now I'm stuck in gray and I'm fighting to bring us into color."

"I know. I'm sorry Kayne," I softly say.

"I don't want you to be sorry, Emmy!" Kayne shouts and jumps up from the sofa bed. "None of it is your fault, but you *need* to let me in. I just crawled through the last five years of my life. I want to get back up on my feet, or at least to my knees and start rebuilding my life with you."

Kayne takes two steps, kneels down in front of me, and cups my cheeks with his big, soft hands. Tears fall fast from my pained eyes.

"Baby, I'm sorry. I don't want to make you

cry," he says softly as he wipes away my tears with this thumbs.

Warmth surrounds me, sweeping through my veins. My body recognizes it. The beautiful sensation reminds me I'm safe; I'm loved, and reassures me that one day I may be okay.

I meet Kayne 's eyes and I crack. I love this man. I want this man. *Reach out and take him!* I do. I ignore the screaming in my mind to keep away and my arms reach out and around Kayne 's neck.

As I pull him close, I hear Kayne 's sharp intake of breath. My heart's racing as I press my lips hard against his. The pressure is only coming from me as he is stone still. It's just one, hard, long closed-lip kiss.

I pull back breathless, adrenaline shoots through my body and I feel as if I could do anything right now.

Our eyes meet, and I watch as a shocked Kayne stares back at me. His eyes flare with hope and that's all it takes for me to bring him close to me again.

This time Kayne 's hands move to my waist and grip me tightly. He picks me up and I wrap my legs around his hips as our mouths clash together in a hard, hungry, painful kiss. Our teeth clash and we bite each other's lips.

Kayne lays me down on the sofa bed gently, careful not to break the kiss. Our hands are everywhere. I'm digging my hands into his ass and Kayne 's fingers are making a slow perusal under my top and up to my breasts. When his warm hands cup my breasts, I sigh into his mouth. *Bliss.* We stay like this for what feels like hours, but is probably only minutes. When we need to breathe, Kayne breaks the kiss and moves his lips along my jaw and down my neck. "Emmy," he whispers over and over again against my skin. Then he takes my lips again and everything disappears except the feeling of Kayne 's soft, wet lips on mine, and his warm calloused hands gliding along my skin.

Kayne releases my lips again and our heavy breaths echo around the room. He kisses along my jaw and down to my neck.

Abruptly a powerful flash of a faceless man appears in my mind. *His hands wound tight around my neck.* My breathing accelerates.

Kayne 's head darts up from my neck and searches my face. *The faceless man is laughing. His grip on my throat tightens.* I bring my hands up trying to free myself so I can breathe.

"Emmy, baby. What's wrong?"

Hands to my neck and with crazed eyes, I stare at Kayne. Panic flashes on his face as he realizes I'm stuck in a memory that's grabbed hold of me and isn't letting me go. Kayne 's eyes dart to my hands rubbing on my throat.

"Emmy, no one's hurting you, baby. It's just you and me here. No one is ever going to hurt you again. I promise."

The faceless man continues to laugh and mock me. I clench my eyes closed and feel them squeeze out tears. They roll down the sides of my face and hit my ears.

"Emmy, you need to breathe. You are in control. Breathe in through your nose and out your mouth, now."

Still with closed eyes, I try to follow Kayne 's instructions, but I only end up blowing big puffs out through my mouth in my panicked state to try and calm down.

I feel warmth envelop my face and then Kayne 's whispered voice is right at my ear, "In through your nose, baby, out through your mouth." His gentle and calm tone has me focused on him and I follow his directions.

Inhale.

Exhale.

Inhale.

Exhale.

With each breath, Kayne repeats his words in

the same gentle voice.

The fog begins to clear and I open my eyes. It takes a moment, but Kayne and the room come into focus. He gently moves my hands from my neck and kisses both my wrists.

I fall apart right in front of him. Sobs rip from my chest and I turn to my side and curl into my body. *A kiss, I can't even kiss without these hideous memories assaulting me.*

Kayne lies beside me and pulls me into his body. I feel the vibration of my cries through his chest onto my face. He's silent as his strong arms hold me tightly. I sense him flinch every time another harrowing cry escapes my throat.

A little while later, I've calmed down, or is it that my body just has nothing left? Perhaps my tears have finally abandoned me again. I've been here before, my body giving up and setting straight to numb.

Two soft fingers grip my chin and force my head up. I close my eyes tightly. I don't want to see his face. What if he's disappointed, disgusted or thinks I'm insane. I can't handle this.

"Emmy, please open your eyes." I clench them closed tighter, hearing the pain in his voice.

"I love you, Emily. Nothing you could ever do will change that. Don't shy away from me now, baby. We just had a beautiful moment. Remember the good, forget the bad." *So easy for him to say.*

I open my eyes. With a furrowed brow and pressed lips, Kayne stares back at me. I think of making a joke about worry lines, but decide against it. His face relaxes and he kisses my forehead. He looks back to my eyes and doesn't release them while he speaks.

"I fucking adore you more than life itself, Emmy. If you go into the dark again, you tell me. Because I'll always be here to pull you out. Out into the bright light, where you belong."

I don't say anything. I hold his stare for a moment longer and then curl into his body. Kayne pulls the covers over us and hugs me tightly to his chest.

This is wrong and I shouldn't stay lying here with him but I need this. *Just one night.* I did exactly what I said I wouldn't. He got close and now he's seen a small part of me, an ugly part of my life I didn't want anyone ever to see. It's only a matter of time before he understands I'm too far gone and he doesn't want to be a part of my dark world. People can only take so much before they walk away. They will see I'm not worth the effort, and then, I'll know; I lost them because they saw just how ugly I have become.

My stomach churns, but it's not my tummy. It's anger swirling around my scarred soul. Rage. Now more than ever, I need to reach Donovan. And when I do, I may not make it out alive, but neither will he.

Death while seizing my revenge seems fitting. He helped create me and I shall destroy us both.

Chapter Thirteen

I woke up early this morning and crawled out of Kayne 's arms and off the sofa bed easily. Kayne 's always been a heavy sleeper. I stayed watching him sleep a bit. He looks so peaceful. His hair mussed, face soft and slightly pouty lips. He really is the most handsome man I've ever seen.

An hour later and I'm in the dining room trying to figure out what I'm going to do when I focus on the pictures of Lily and Jake on the table.

They're beautiful together and it has nothing to do with looks; it's how their love for each other shines through their eyes. Just one look and the whole world can see how much they mean to each other. My brother's arms are wrapped around Lily possessively. He's going to protect her forever. Lily's smile up at Jake says how happy she is, how she's going to make my brother happy forever.

"As hard as it sounds, you need to let go of the

past and embrace your future."

Argh. How is it my past when it affects me every day? Just last night. That's my present and that's why it's always going to be my future. I need control; that's what I need to do. I need to step back from Kayne or I'm going to hurt him more. I love him, so much, but he's going to want things I can't give him, children, to become a family, but I can't do that. I'm too damaged to ever become a mother. My future holds me being alone. I'm doomed to watch as Kayne receives that gift from another woman. My heart splinters, but it's the only way.

My head whips as I hear footsteps. I see Kayne walk into the entry hall from the living room. He sees me and then pins me with his eyes and there's fire there. I know why. I remember.

"Emmy, I'm pretty sure you haven't forgotten this, but I will remind you just in case. I fucking hate waking up and finding you gone from the bed. That has not changed, just to be clear," Kayne says with raised eyebrows.

He takes a step toward the dining room and I raise my hand, "Stop."

Kayne freezes on the spot and narrows his eyes on me.

"Last night was amazing and," I pause to find the right word, "scary," I say softly. "But it was a

123

onetime thing. I'm sorry if I led you on to think it would move you and me to an *us*, because it won't. I need you to know it won't happen again."

Kayne stays silent for a moment while his eyes continue to pierce mine. Then he abruptly laughs.

My brows drop as I'm trying to figure out what the hell he thinks is funny.

Kayne steps toward me and I take a step back.

"Emmy, this is what's going to happen. I'm moving back in. This," Kayne points his finger between him and me, "is happening. Fuck, I've been waiting for you to make the first move for three goddamn months and last night you did; that's all I needed. I know you want me. I know you love me. Now it's my move and, baby, I'm taking a huge fucking step right into your life and there is nothing you can do about it. You're mine, always have been. Only sweet days ahead for us, Emmy. I'm going to show you that."

Shock radiates through me and my mouth dries up like the Sahara desert. My lips part but no sound comes out. I shake my head, trying to signal to Kayne that this is not happening. *This is your Kayne. How could you not realize this is what he would do?* That thought alone stops my head shaking. I should have known. I do know. Nothing is going to stop Kayne from moving back in, and I have no money to move out. *You don't want to.* No, I don't. Goddamn, I'm weak. I want this. I want him. I just need to fight harder. Fight harder for his future.

Kayne steps up to me and cups my cheek. He's smiling. A full, bright smile. The first I've seen in five years. My thoughts and doubts come to a halt. I melt into his hand and stare at his beautiful smile.

"For never was a story of more woe than this of Juliet and her Romeo," Kayne softly whispers before he gently kisses my closed lips. "That's us, baby, but we win. We turn our nightmares into a beautiful dream."

And with those devastating beautiful words that I want to come true so badly, Kayne turns and leaves the house.

I'm still staring at the door when I hear his truck leave the driveway and drive to where, I'm not sure. Then I'm zapped out of my bubble realizing he's probably gone to Dom's to retrieve his things. *Damn it!*

***

I'm sitting in my therapist's room watching her jot down her notes as I've just told her about my night with Kayne and explained how impossible the man is, and that he's now moving in. She smirked. *Everyone is against me!*

"So what made you want to kiss Kayne last night?"

I'm used to her direct questions by now. If a person off the street asked me personal questions, I'd have been shocked and I would imagine slapping them in my mind. Only in my mind, though. I could never actually hit a person just over words. Donovan on the other hand, well, that man has a whole world of hurt coming his way. Let's see how much he likes me when I'm not locked in a room with only a bed and a huge man guarding the door.

"Emily?" I hear Dr. Zeek say, trying to grab my attention.

"Umm, sorry, what was the question again?"

"How about we talk about what was just on your mind?"

"I was thinking about Donovan. About what I would do to him if I wasn't locked in a room."

"Okay, and what would you do?"

"Torture and kill him," I say without having to think for even a second.

"Hmm." Dr. Zeek begins jotting down more notes.

I sigh, "Why don't you buy a recorder instead of writing it all down?" I've wondered this during every session. It would save her a lot of time and probably arthritis in her wrists.

"Because I only need to remember the important parts. Now, why would you rather torture and kill Donovan instead of sending him to prison for the rest of his life?"

My breath stalls and I gasp Dr. Zeek with astonishment. "That would be too kind. Plus, there's no way to say that would happen. What he did, he did in another country. The places and evidence are gone, burned to the ground. He would get off and do this to someone else. I can't let that happen. I'm not going to let that happen," I end with a shout, moving to the front of my chair, my chest rising and falling fast.

"You say it like you are doing something about that, Emily. Are you?"

I dart my eyes straight to the window while I shake my head. I'm desperately trying to think of something to say when I hear her inhale sharply and my eyes dart straight back to her.

"Emily, I know the signs when people are lying to lie to me. This is what I went to college for eight years for. What are you into? What are you thinking? You barely escaped alive last time and you are trying to find this man?" she asks her questions quickly and panic is leaked all over her words.

"I found him," I state and decide since I can't lie to her, I will be honest. I know she can't tell anyone what we talk about, only under oath in court. "He's been looking for me, and eventually he will find me. I'm going to catch him before he gets to me. Before he can come anywhere near my family, near Kayne. "

"That sounds dangerous, Emily, and what you're willing to do is going to change you more than you already have. Taking someone's life, there is no coming back from that."

"He's not even a person. He's a thing. I will only feel relief. I'll be saving countless other women."

"That's where you're wrong, Emily. You will feel guilt. The relief you are so desperate for can only come from you learning to love your scarred soul. Killing Donovan will only compound your conscience and make it worse. This isn't who you were or who you are, Emily."

I shake my head repeatedly, not wanting to hear her words. I understand what I will feel. I will be saving others. That's all I need to know. Dr. Zeek wasn't there. She can't fathom how much of a monster he is just from the words she hears me say about him.

I stand from the chair. "I'm done for today. See

you on Wednesday." With those words, I leave her office and her warnings behind.

***

Pulling into my driveway, I see Kayne 's truck and I spot his feet crossed and resting on the porch. I park behind his car and hop out. I slam my car door shut and see his head pop around the porch barrier. He's on a phone call. His eyes bore into me, the heat and intensity from his stare has me rubbing my thighs together. *No! Get a hold of yourself, Emily.* Do not lead him in the wrong direction. Into a direction of never having a family and never truly being happy.

I walk up the steps and past him. All the while, he keeps his eyes on me. They travel my body slowly up and down. *God, I need to stay away from him.* I practically fall over my feet running into the house.

I walk through the entry to the dining room and notice my pictures are gone, not gone, stacked on top of each other and put in a pile on the cabinet in the dining room.

My chest constricts. I drop my bag to the floor, grab my pictures and spread them out on the table. First picture, Lily and Jake, Second picture, older lady walking past my house, third picture, a young man skating past the shops, fourth picture a teenage girl walking with her friends.

I sense Kayne enter the room watching me closely while I furiously place out my pictures.

"Emmy, I'm making dinner. I moved them so we would have room to eat."

I don't ignore Kayne. I just can't do anything until I have all my pictures placed back out on the table. There are answers to my questions in these pictures. I need them kept out. I need to look them over. I need them left alone.

"Emily?"

I place the last picture on one of the chairs, as there is no room left on the table. I examine the last picture. It's of a couple I spotted walking out of my therapist's office. I followed them downstairs and almost missed my appointment all because I needed to capture their picture. For some reason, they need help with something, yet hand in hand, they walk out smiling. *How?* I'm lost in my own world when I feel Kayne 's warm hand on my elbow.

I snap out of my thoughts and look straight at him.

"Emmy, are you ignoring me?"

"No, I just need these pictures out at all times. Please don't stack them again. When I'm ready, I will put them away. But that time is not yet, okay?"

"Baby, have you told Dr. Zeek about your pictures?"

I focus on Kayne confused. Why would I tell her I take pictures?

"Emmy, these," he pushes his hand out to the pictures, "are a result of what you went through."

"It's fine, Kayne. Really, this phase of mine will pass." I walk out of the dining room before he can reply. The pictures are for me. They are a puzzle I need to work out. Dr. Zeek can't help me with that.

I spot a tossed salad on the bench and steaks cooking on the grill. I inhale deeply when I smell the marinade. Kayne used to make it all the time for me. It was my favorite. I used to think about it in the collection house. When I was bored, I would try to re-create it, but could never achieve exactly the same result, or maybe I had just forgotten how it tasted.

Heat hits my back. I step forward and turn around. "Barbecue marinated steaks, hey?"

"I wanted to make you one of your favorites to celebrate us being back in our house tonight."

I sigh heavily. "Kayne," I say in a warning tone. "Nothing has changed between us. You may be forcing your way back into my life, but it's not because I asked you into it." The words are harsh and they sting as they pass my lips. I was never this cruel before. God, I don't want to be this person.

"Oh, baby, we have changed. Maybe not as

much as I'd have liked to by now, but for now, it's enough. Now why don't you go have a shower or bath? Dinner's in thirty." With that, Kayne goes to the grill and flips the steaks.

I know there's no use fighting him on this. He knows where I stand. I know he will keep pushing and I need to be ready for those moments. To save him, I will deny myself what I want. In time, he will see I did what's best for him.

Facing off against Donovan also looms over me. I may not come out alive, another reason to keep my distance from Kayne.

Chapter Fourteen

I woke up in bed this morning still feeling full from the marinated steaks last night. They were as delicious as I remember them. Kayne and I ate in comfortable silence, and then we both silently cleaned up together. Kayne did the dishes and I dried. It was eerie, just what we used to do, only no touching, kissing and laughing. I could almost hear the echoes of our laughter through the silence. Kayne glanced my way many times, his intense stares on my skin, begging me to turn to him and what, smile, be the old Emily? I went to bed right after the last plate was dry. Kayne had finished washing and stood against the bench watching me. I had to get out of there. The old familiar sensation of heat was building between my legs, my body vibrating with need for him.

Now, I'm sitting in Kayne's truck wearing denim shorts and a white blouse, my camera around my neck and Kayne and I are on our way to Jake and Lily's house. Jake called early this morning and asked us to come. He wouldn't tell us why, just said to get our butts over to his place by ten am.

When we arrive, I see my parents' car there along with Nick and Dom's cars.

"When did Dom arrive back?" I ask Kayne.

"Two days ago. His mission was unsuccessful and he won't tell anyone why."

"What does unsuccessful mean?"

"Either they found out he was uncover or he quit the mission. I'm not sure which one it is yet, but ever since he's been back, he's been an asshole. So I'm thinking he was found out. Which is dangerous if they find out who he really is."

I rub my arms as goose bumps rise on my skin. I've known Dom since I was a little girl. I've known all the boys that long. Jake, Kayne, Dom and Nick have been inseparable their whole lives. Dom is the more dangerous one out of them all. He lives for dangerous situations, always has, from racing streetcars to battling in underground fights. But he always came out on top; it's just who he is. He's one of those lucky guys. No matter what he does, he comes out on top. I guess, you can't be lucky forever.

We knock, but there's no answer so Kayne tries the door handle and finds it unlocked. We walk in and the house is silent, so we head for the back door. We step outside to the back porch and find everyone out there, everyone but Lily. Jake sees us and practically runs over. He picks me up and hugs me tightly.

"There's my little sister."

I press my face into his shoulder and inhale. He smells like my brother, like home. I hug him tightly, wishing I never had to let go. My brother is so happy. I've never seen him this cheerful in all my life. I've seen him with plenty of girls before, but not like this, not content and at peace with himself and the world.

He places me down and kisses my cheek. "How's my sis?" he asks softly.

"I'm good," I say back.

Jake pulls back and looks down at me. "Still a way to go, Em, but I believe you will get there."

My heart stops almost instantly. How can everyone keep seeing through me? I'm trying my hardest to fool them and yet it's never enough. I just nod slowly and try to change the subject, which is easy when I mention the one person Jake can't help but lose himself in.

"Where's Lily?"

Jake's smile widens to impossible lengths and answers, "I asked her to go to the Mall to pick us up some lunch."

"Okay, what's with the huge smile, big brother? You're starting to freak me out."

"You'll see, little sis. Just don't go anywhere, okay?" he says sternly, still smiling like a fool.

"Okay, jeez, not like I have any other place to be," I say sarcastically.

I look up and see everyone staring at me. Kayne and my father are grinning. Jake and my mother's eyes are wide and Nick and Dom both have their mouths hanging wide open in shock. Then I realized too late. I had a small smile on my face. I lost the smile and missed catching it. Everyone comes over and gives me a hug, telling me how well I'm doing.

"Even more reason to celebrate," I hear my brother say.

The pressure to get better and be fixed weighs heavily on my soul. These are only small changes and I can't promise I will ever be any better than what I am right now.

Half an hour later, my mother comes running out of Jake's house like a lunatic, screaming, "She's here! She's here!"

"Jesus, Mom, keep it down. She's going to think something bad is happening hearing you scream like that," Jake admonishes her.

I quirk an eyebrow at them, feeling left out of

the loop.

I peer up to Kayne, who's standing beside me smiling. So it appears he knows or he's just finding my mother and brother hilarious, which isn't hard to do when it's my mother. She's unique to put it mildly. She's excited easily and finds friends everywhere. Shops, restaurants, and movies, anywhere really, my mother will find someone to talk with for hours. Many shopping trips I've sat my butt down on a seat while my mom talked the ear off a sales assistant.

I look around and find my dad, Dom and Nick all with big grins as well. I stomp my foot. *Yes, stomped my foot.*

"Why I am the only one who doesn't know what's happening?"

Kayne answers me, "Baby, he didn't tell any of us, but we've guessed. Think about it, Emmy, all the family is here. He's surprising Lily. What do you think he's going to do? Dump her?"

My eyes go wide and I look around to Jake as Lily walks out the back door. My brother gets down on one knee and extends his arms up with a ring box in his hands. I grab hold of Kayne 's hand tightly to hold me up. *He's proposing.* My brother is asking Lily to marry him.

I release Kayne 's arm and quickly grasp my

camera from around my neck and start taking pictures.

Lily and Jake's smiles light up the backyard.

"Lily Morgan, you are the most beautiful woman I have ever laid eyes on. Your strength has built the roads we are travelling on and they are smooth because you never give up."

"Your brother is closing the hole more and more every day with his love and support."

"I want to wake up and go to sleep next to you for the rest of my life. I want to keep showing you the best of me." Tears fall from Lily's eyes and she covers her mouth with her hand. But you can tell she's smiling from the creases beside her wet eyes. "Your strong spirit and sassy attitude have me addicted to you, Lil. It would be an honor and a blessing to be able to create a life and a family with you. You breathe life into me, baby. So, Lily Morgan, will you make me the happiest man alive and marry me?"

Lily releases her hand from her mouth and screams, "Yes!" Taking the ring, she jumps straight into Jake's arms and they kiss.

Click, smile, *click,* laugh, *click,* kiss, *click,* smile, *click,* they are so happy.

I feel a gentle touch on my shoulder and glance up to see it's Kayne. I look around and find everyone watching me. I must have gone a bit crazy with the pictures. Jake and Lily are still too lost in each other to notice.

My dad walks up to me and puts his arm around my shoulders. He's warm and comforting. I lay my head on his shoulder and he kisses my hair.

My mom rushes to Lily and Jake to congratulate them. Same with Nick, Dom and Kayne. All with back pats for Jake and hugs for Lily.

Dad kisses my hair, long and hard, then releases me and goes to Lily, giving her a tight hug. Her face crumbles a little and then my mom joins in and I watch as tears fall from Lily's eyes. Yeah, my parents have the best hugs. I know how much Lily appreciates them; anyone would after losing their own parents.

My mom and dad release her and tell her how happy they are that she will be joining our family. Lily's eyes sparkle with excitement, yet she has a small smile and she's rubbing her hands together roughly.

Jake wraps his arms around her, causing Lily to release her clutched hands. Her shoulders relax. The anxiety disappears and a content look washes over her.

Hmm, so love, it's love that gives you that

feeling; the sensation that everything is going to be okay. I know this. I look over at Kayne talking to Dom. I know that feeling. I remember it.

For a split second, I think maybe I can't feel it because I don't love Kayne anymore, but I know it's not about Kayne feeling my love; it's about me accepting his. I haven't felt love in five years. Have I forgotten how to appreciate it, how to receive it?

I turn away from them all and furrow my forehead as I rack my brain for those moments.

Kayne hugging me my first day of college. I was so nervous. One hug and I knew everything would be okay, because no matter what, I had him.

Before my final exams. A long hard hug from Kayne and I knew I was going to do my best and that's all I could do.

My first day of teaching. One hug from Kayne and I knew everything would turn out just fine.

Kayne walks into my line of sight. His eyes are narrowed at me, as if he knows what I'm thinking.

"Emmy."

I scan the yard for an escape, while shaking my head furiously. I'm on the edge of falling apart in front of everyone I care about.

"Emmy, don't shut it out. Those emotions you're feeling, you need to experience them, to open your wounds and let them bleed so you can move on. You keep closing those emotions off, but you need to acknowledge them so you can move forward."

"Please," I beg. "Not here. I don't want my family seeing how messed up I still am."

"Oh, baby, when will you realize they can see it written all over you when you're pretending to be someone you aren't."

I look up to Kayne furious. "I'm not pretending to be anyone," I seethe. "This is me, Kayne. That's what *you* don't get."

I turn away from him, calm myself, and walk to Lily and Jake, who are still talking to my parents.

"Congratulations you two," I say and hug them both. "Look after my brother," I whisper into Lily's ear.

"Always," she whispers back to me.

I say my goodbyes to everyone. My parents give me tight hugs and both whisper to me how happy they are that I'm doing so well. The cuts on my thighs choose that moment to throb, mocking me. I hug them back and then walk quickly through the house. I come to the front yard and see Kayne 's truck. I came with him. Footsteps come from behind me. I turn to see Dom.

"Leaving so soon, hey?" he says with a raised eyebrow and a grin on his lips.

"I was until I remembered Kayne drove me here. Care to help a girl out and give me a ride home?"

Dom huffs out a laugh. "And have the wrath of Kayne for taking you home, no way."

I sigh. Great. I'll just walk then. It's not far from to house. I peer down the road and then a sliver of fear creeps up my spine as I see the isolated street with no people around. I think I might wait for Kayne.

"Emmy, I can't begin to understand what you went through, but I want you to know, if you need to talk to someone, I'm always here."

I nod. "Thanks, Dom, appreciate that, but I'm okay. Doing well," I say with as much strength as I can.

Dom's face goes soft and he gives me a smile. "You always did suck at lying, Em, but damn, you have actually gotten worse at it. Just do me one favor, hey?"

I narrow my eyes at him when yet again another person in my life can read me like a book; open me up and see all the gory and gruesome details.

I press my lips tightly together and nod.

"When you finally feel that smile before it happens." He points to the corner of my mouth where I felt the smile earlier. "Grab hold of it and don't let go. Remember why you smiled, store it, and repeat it again and again until smiling becomes effortless."

I nod slowly. My eyes sting but I refuse to let any tears fall. Why can't they be blind to my pain? Why can't they not care?

Because you are loved. Grab hold of it and don't let go.

Chapter Fifteen

Dom's phone rings. He looks to the screen and his eyes narrow, his face growing angry. Giving me a hug, he walks quickly to his car and drives off with spinning wheels and a screech. I shake my head. That's just Dom. He's wild. I hope he finds a girl one day who can settle him down, if not, she will need to match his wild ways.

I take a seat on the front steps of my brother's house. It's not long after Dom leaves that I sense him behind me. Watching me for a long moment, I pretend I don't realize he's there and then he speaks. "Let's go." Kayne stalks past me. I stand and walk after him. We climb into his truck and are silent the whole drive home.

When we arrive, I jump out and dash up the steps and unlock the front door. I want to jump into the shower and avoid the explosive conversation I can see growing inside Kayne.

I open the door, walk in and when my foot is on the first step, Kayne 's hand grips my elbow and turns me toward him.

His face is soft but it's fixed with a determination.

"No matter what twisted game your mind is playing on you, *always* remember I'm here and I'm not going anywhere. You decide to let those negative feelings you have for yourself out, let me know. I'll be here before and after you've told me what you really think of yourself."

He doesn't get it. "Kayne, look at us. Yet another argument, another time I'm standing here rejecting you. I'm a lost cause. I'm too far gone. I can't overcome this. It's too much, too hard. The more time you spend with me, the more you're going to see how ugly I have become. You live your life through days, weeks, and years. Moments, moments are all I have. Getting from one to the next is exhausting. I want you to remember me as the strong and proud Emily, but you keep seeing me fall down. There is only so much you will take before you want to leave this nightmare behind. You'll beg me to let you go."

"Never," he fires back straight away. "Whatever you think of yourself, I think the exact opposite. I wish you could see yourself through my eyes. You are my strong, proud, and beautiful

Emily. No matter distance, time or personality changes we go through, you are mine and I am yours. I'm sick of fighting it. I'm sick of waiting to claim what has always been mine, what will always be mine."

Rattled to the core, I'm once again shocked by his words. That's what it will be then, left for him to find out on his own. And when he leaves, I will know it's because he saw what has grown and festered for so long, my ugly, scarred soul.

Kayne takes in my resigned expression and cups my cheek.

"Baby, I love the woman inside here." He touches my chest over my heart. "I love her spirit, her sarcastic nature, her fucking beautiful positivity. And although you haven't shown those things, I know they are in there."

"Walk away, Kayne. Just leave me be and don't look back," I whisper; however, at the same time, I turn my face into his comforting hand. I'm begging him to leave, but my body is unable to let him go.

"I can't," he says softly. "And I never will. I'm here through thick and thin. I'm here to save that beautiful, bruised soul of yours."

I finally let my tears go and sobs soon follow. Kayne catches me as I fall to the stairs. He cradles me in his arms as I say over and over again, "You will leave. You will leave. You will leave. And then I won't have a soul at all."

Kayne rocks me and matches my repeated words, "I love you. I love you. I love you. I'll save your soul."

A small icicle breaks off from my heart. I try to catch it before it falls, but it shatters into a million pieces. That small part of my heart is exposed and the pain is excruciating. Slithers of emotions seep in through the gap. He loves me. He will understand. He will always love me. *Until he sees me for who I really am.* Doubt creeps in and washes over me repeatedly until my breath is stolen and I'm drowning in it. *I can't risk it. I've lost too much of myself already.*

I push away from Kayne and quickly climb the stairs. I race into my room, rip my clothes from my body, and climb into the shower. I sink to the floor and cry into the water.

Echoes of my broken heart surround me in the small bathroom. I wonder if God is watching, he knows what he has done to me. What his decided fate has put me through. I beg him to give a reprieve, to give me hope.

***

Kayne

I watch as the love of my life runs from me yet again. But I won't let her. I follow her up the stairs and watch as she strips her clothes, rushes into the shower and drops her body to the floor, crying into the water.

Her sobs echo around the room. My lungs constrict and I struggle to breathe at hearing my girl in so much pain.

Every day she fights me, I fail. This is my purpose on earth, to be with this woman, protect her, and create a life where she can be happy, but I've failed.

I sink to the floor, my back against the wall next to the shower and I place my hand on the glass where Emmy rests her body.

I sit, touching the glass that's touching the love of my life and pray to God to give her strength and courage to keep fighting her demons. And to give me the strength to keep saving her.

I bow my head, while my palm stays flat to her back. I take in every cry. I take it on. I inhale her pain, hoping it gives her a lighter burden to carry around.

Her cries slow and almost stop. I want to think it's because she can feel me here, but I don't dare get my hopes up.

***

Emily

After being in the shower for a long time. I turn the water off and turn around expecting to see Kayne there. I swear I could feel him in the room with me. Maybe my prayers were answered and God zapped me with a last dose of strength to help me get through a moment I felt would never end. *But what about the next moment.*

I exit the shower and wrap a towel around my body. My mind screams at me to cut. *No!* I grab hold of the bench and push my palms down painfully hard. *Let this be enough. Please, don't go there again.* I push down on the bench harder, a sharp cramp runs through my hands and up my arms. I let go of the bench and rub my palms together. I stare down at the draw I know holds the shavers. My fingers itch to open the draw and pick one up.

My reflection in the mirror catches my eyes. My pathetic, worthless self-staring back at me.

"You worthless piece of shit. As if any other man would want you anyway. You're used goods. Nobody wants dirty second hand trash.

I pull at my hair and hiss to the mirror. "Stop it! You aren't here. You don't control me anymore."

Without one more single thought, I open the

draw and pick out a shaver. I snap the plastic away. Cutting my thumb in the process, but I don't feel the cut, I only see it. I pull the razor free and run my cut thumb over the blade, slicing my cut even deeper. I breathe out with relief. I control this cut. It's mine and mine alone to create, to heal or to keep cutting deeper.

I take a step back and sit on the toilet lid. I pull the towel up and lean my foot on the shower glass window. I bend my knee to the side slightly and there they are, out in the open, all my cuts. Three long lines.

I point the blade side on ready to cut down the second line. I slice the end of the sore open, and as soon as I feel the skin part my pulse races and my mind clears, but it doesn't last long. I watch as blood bubbles to the surface and shame rolls through me like a tidal wave. Usually, this is where I keep cutting to keep the feeling of my heart accelerating and my mind clearing. However, this time the shame is like thunder rumbling through my body. My hands tremble. My throat grows thick and I hear roaring in my ears from my pounding heart. Shame, I'm filled with it.

What am I doing? What have I done to myself? I'm letting the devil win. *I'm helping him.* At that moment, the bathroom door opens and I'm frozen. The door doesn't even open fast, it opens painstakingly slowly, to the point I'm screaming in my mind to hide the blade, to hide the scars, but part of me, a stronger part than my mind wants to get caught, wants to be found out.

But I'm not ready for the hurt and fear that crosses his features. That look has my leg lowering and me cowering on the floor in between the toilet and the shower, hiding myself, hiding my secret. Praying he disappears, knowing he won't, but still stupidly hoping.

Silence stretches on for what feels like forever. It's torture. I wish to hear the door slam shut as Kayne realizes how far gone and broken I truly am.

The slam never comes. Instead, his strong, warm arms pick me up and carry me to the bed where he sits me in his lap as he leans against the headboard and he cries into my neck.

His gruff voice vibrates through my body. "Hold me, Emmy. Hold me so I don't destroy everything in this fucking room."

With shaking hands, I drop the razor to the bed and wrap my arms around his body. Kayne 's silent tears fall on my naked shoulders.

Sitting in this position with Kayne, I realize yet again that I am the reason he's hurting. Yet, the weight of it doesn't fall hard on my shoulders like it did before. My mind instantly goes to Marco,

Donovan and all those faceless men which have blurred into one. *They* are why Kayne is hurting. *They* created this woman I have become. I'm just not strong enough to fight the downward spiral I'm on. *That's a lie. You've fought the spiral for five years.* Did I? I think I may have, barely, but I've come out weak, useless. I need to find my strength again. I need to dig deep.

I pull back from Kayne, a sudden urge to see Dr. Zeek comes over me. "I need to see my therapist," I announce.

He lifts his face to mine and my heart dies as I take in his red-rimmed, glassy eyes.

"I'm so sorry," I whisper. "Please know I *am* trying." I shake my head. "No, I am going to start trying, I realize what I've done to myself is wrong, and I'm going to try and stop," I say softly.

I track a lone tear that falls from Kayne 's eye and a sob rips from my chest. I promise myself in that moment, he will never see me this weak again. Because I can't bear to see him this tortured ever again.

Chapter Sixteen

I'm catching the elevator up to Dr. Zeek's office. I don't have an appointment. I hope she's here. I need to see her.

The elevator doors ding open and I jog through the hall and push open the glass doors to the reception area. The receptionist, Amy, sees me and smiles brightly.

"Emily, how are you? I didn't know you were in today. Did you switch days?"

"I need to see Dr. Zeek, today, now. Is that possible? Please say that's possible," I plead.

"Well," she drags out the word and I tap my finger on her desk in impatience. She holds a finger up to me and says, "Hang tight for one minute, lovely."

I nod and watch as she picks up her phone and after a short moment speaks, "Emily Roberts is here to see you and it seems she's in need of a session right now." Amy pauses, "Okay."

She hangs up the phone and I look in her eyes, eager to see the response in her expression; however, she's quicker and tells me first.

"She said to go right in."

"Thank you," I say.

She gives me a bright smile and I hope one day my smile can be as bright as Amy's.

I open the door to Dr. Zeek's office and find her at her desk, eating a sandwich. She must be on a break.

"Damn, I'm sorry. I can wait out in the reception and let you finish that," I say, but my eyes are begging her to tell me to stay.

"Nonsense, I can eat and listen. Take a seat, Emily, and tell me why you felt you needed to see me urgently. Has something happened?"

"I'm cutting my skin," I blurt out before I lose my courage. I'm expecting to see shock, panic, judgment on her face, but all I see is a soft woman's soft, understanding face.

"And why do you think you cut, Emily?" she asks, not missing a beat.

"When my memories and thoughts are too overwhelming, I cut to free my mind. Cutting clears my thoughts and gives me a moment of peace."

"And after?"

"Shame, disgust," I whisper, but still loud enough for her to hear me.

"And what made you come here to tell me today?"

What did? When I cut myself today, I already knew I'd gone too far. I wanted to stop. "Part of it was when I cut today, the shame, the feeling of knowing what I had done to my flesh. And the other part, the part which pushed me to actually do this, Kayne caught me. Well, for once, I think I wanted to be found out, so I didn't hide it. Until I saw his reaction and then I felt disgusted with myself. He picked me up and cried with me. He's hurting and I don't want to ever do that to him again." I take a long breath in. "I need help. I need you to help me to be strong again."

"What makes you think you aren't strong?"

My forehead creases while I stare at Dr. Zeek, trying to figure out if this is a trick question.

She throws her leftover sandwich in the bin under her desk and walks over to the seat I'm on and sits next to me.

"Emily, before you were kidnapped, I wouldn't have called you unique. I would have called you normal, average. You lived a normal, average life, but because of the unfortunate events that have happened to you, you are now unique. Why? Because you survived the impossible. Every day you walk around living; you are surviving. And every day you fight your feelings to not be with the man you love, because you think you're saving him, makes you unique, but most of all, you are strong. All of those things take strength."

I shake my head. "No, I gave up. I gave into them. I ended up letting them do those things to me. I became weak," I shout and stand from the sofa, wanting distance from this woman and her words. Words I'm desperate to believe.

Dr. Zeek looks up to me with intent in her eyes. "Don't you see, Emily, you've never been weak. A weak person would have ended their life during or after your kidnapping. But you haven't, won't, because you are strong. You're a survivor."

Strong, survivor.

"Marco, Donovan, all of those men planted those thoughts in you. They aren't who you are. They are who *they* are."

"Who they are?" *Weak, worthless, used and disgusting.*

"Those men went to those parties looking for women who couldn't escape them because of their insecurities. They only reflected how they felt about themselves onto you because they can't handle what they are or what they have become from previous abuse or being brought up and told that's who they were. They had a choice; to become better than their abuser or to become their abuser. They choose wrong and for that, God will punish them."

Dr. Zeek's words spin around in my mind. I know what she's saying is the truth. I saw the disgust on their faces, the hatred they had for me yet they didn't even know me.

The realization of what Dr. Zeek is explaining spreads through my body. I believe those men thought that way about themselves, so then I have to ask myself, am I like those men? No. Never. I'm nothing like them.

So how do I move on with that knowledge? I've defined myself as weak and worthless for so long. If I'm not those, than what am I? I don't feel strong and I don't feel happy, so where do I go from here?

***

Kayne

The desire to hit something, hurt someone is thundering through my body. From the tips of my toes to the tingling in my fingertips, I need to cause some damage.

My Emmy, with a razor to her beautiful soft skin is repeating over in my mind and I'm going to go crazy if my fists don't hit something soon.

I turn into Dom's place and break quickly. The tires screech and the car slides for about a meter.

I jump out of the car, leaving the keys and not bothering to shut my door. I push open the side gate and it hits the fence, flying back at me, but I'm ready and I force it back again. I reach around to my neck, pull my shirt up, and throw it to the ground.

I hear Dom calling my name but I ignore him. I'm only here for one reason. It's not to see him. I spot what I want and walk straight towards it, rage driving my arm back.

One swing and my fist connects hard with the punching bag. Hard swings, one after another, brutal and fast.

Dom calls out behind me. "Jesus, Kayne, put the fucking gloves on so you don't cut up your knuckles."

I ignore him.

The vision of Emmy cutting, bleeding, crying, drowning, has tainted my vision red. I'm not stopping for gloves. If she's hurting, then so am I.

My girl is hurting. My girl is breaking apart. My girl is hiding away.

I need to save her. I can. I will. I'll die trying.

***

Emily

When I arrived home from my visit with Dr. Zeek the house was empty, no sign of Kayne. If I still knew him at all, he was out letting off some steam.

I'm curled up on the sofa watching TV when I hear his truck drive up. I don't move, just wait for him to come inside. When I hear the door open and close, I glance up and over at the handsome man staring back at me. He walks over and takes a seat next to me on the sofa.

I mute the TV and for the first time since I've been back, I ask him, "How are you?" I'm ashamed of myself that I'm only now asking him this.

Kayne looks at me with sadness in his eyes; the pain of the day evident on his beautiful, weary face.

"Not good, baby," he whispers, and those softly spoken words may as well be thundering bullets right through my heart.

He sits forward, places his elbows on his knees and covers his face with his hands. I notice his knuckles have cuts and are swollen. He's been to Dom's. *Poor punching bag.*

"Thank you," I say loudly in his direction. His head pops up and looks at me confused.

"For never giving up." I take a deep breath and

159

keep going, "I realized something today. I was believing lies monsters told me. I have these ugly emotions which have been plaguing me for so long. Dr. Zeek has made me question those lies and emotions. I've realized something. How can I be these bad things if a man as wonderful as you wants me and believes in me? So, thank you. I'm not better. I'm not even close, but I'm on a much better road than I was before, because of you."

Kayne sits up and reaches out for my hand. I let him take it. I'm not rejecting him; it only hurts us both, but touching is as far as I can go right now. Emotionally, I'm screwed up. I need to figure out where my head is before I risk putting Kayne through any more grief.

"Emmy, baby, that's amazing. Where do we go from here?" Kayne 's thumb runs over my hand in a comforting gesture.

"I don't know," I whisper and look away.

I feel stupid. We've come this far and I'm still confused. I feel like the girl who keeps going back and forth. I'm drowning in a nightmare I created myself, and I can't stop it. I can't stop myself from pushing away the people I love.

I hear Kayne sigh. My eyes flick back to him. His eyes are closed and he's resting his head on the back of the sofa. I decide this is the best time to head to bed. This conversation can only go downhill from here.

I take my hand from his and Kayne 's eyes open. He doesn't attempt to stop me. He just watches me stand up and head for the stairs while he rests on the sofa. I'm half way up the stairs when he stands and speaks, "You can walk away from our conversations, but you can never walk away from me."

I pause in my retreat and turn to him as he gets to the bottom of the steps, staring up at me.

"We are an unfinished love song is all, Emmy. God's just working on our next set of lyrics." He takes two steps at a time to meet me and kisses my forehead. "Sweet dreams, baby."

Kayne walks down the stairs and then into the kitchen.

I'm left frozen on the steps, my mind and body at war with each other. My body begs me to go after him, but my mind wins. I'm still too weak to reach out and take what I want.

I climb the stairs and head for my room. I pull out my laptop, open my email account and find a new message.

Subject: He's on the move.

Donovan is on his way to the USA. He boarded a flight to New York. I'm on the same flight. He hired an investigator to find you. The investigator is in New York City. From my investigations, he has nothing on you yet, but he's good. It will only be a matter of time before he finds you.

So Donovan is already on his way to me. That was much quicker than I anticipated it would be. No matter, I will be ready. Maybe the answers to who I am lie in dealing with him. Revenge may be what truly sets me free.

Chapter Seventeen

It's been a month since Kayne caught me cutting myself. I haven't cut since. I've felt the need. My body raged at me the first few times I craved to clear my mind of my thoughts and memories. It was an easy way to achieve some peace. But the feeling of letting Kayne down weighs heavier on my heart than the painful memories in my mind.

Kayne and I have been taking each day slowly. We've formed a sort of new friendship. One where Kayne constantly pushes my boundaries with words and touching, and one where I gently step away or ignore him. The man is a mountain of steel when he wants something; there is no budging him.

My resolve is a thin sheet of glass with cracks all the way through it. I'm just waiting for that one moment where it all shatters and I'm lost to it.

I'm sitting at a bar, dressed in a one-shouldered

black short dress with ruched sides and single flutter sleeves. Best of all, I'm drinking vodka and lemonade. Damn, I'd forgotten how good alcohol tasted. And the wonderful warm, tingly feeling it gives as it runs through your body and lightens your mood.

It's Jake and Lily's engagement party. They arrived from Australia four days ago and Mom surprised them with a party to celebrate their engagement. I turn in my chair and look at all the people standing around in the beautifully decorated gold and black function room. Women in stunning dresses and men in trousers and buttoned-up shirts.

My eyes drift over the dance floor, they fall on Lily and Jake swaying, holding each other, and staring into each other's eyes. I'm so happy for my brother. He really did find his one true soul mate.

A man catches my attention when he sits next to me at the bar and smiles brightly at me. With his dark hair and expensive looking suit, the similarities of him and Donovan have me moving away from him instantly. His expression turns to confusion as I retreat backwards and slam into a hard body, a body I know all too well.

One of Kayne 's arms wrap around my waist while the other extends to the bar between the man and me.

I peer up at Kayne but he isn't looking at me. No, he's staring down the man at the bar.

"You need to back the fuck off, now," Kayne growls.

The man stands and mutters angrily as he moves away from the bar.

I sigh. "Kayne, what the heck was that?" I question him not nearly as angry as I should be. No, I'm thankful. Thankful Kayne will get rid of any man who comes near me.

"Don't ask questions you already know the answer to, Emmy. You're mine, every fucker in this room will know that when they come near you."

Jesus, at this point, I'm so confused where Kayne and I stand. I'm trying to save him yet he's desperate to drown with me. I'm not strong enough to actually leave him like I should. Move out of our home. *Our home.* I'm so weak, yet this man loves me at my weakest.

I move out of Kayne 's arms and my body screams at me in protest.

I step up to the bar and down the rest of my drink. I signal the lady behind the bar and ask for another. I think it's my third or fourth?

"Take it easy, Emmy. When was the last time you had a drink? Have you even had a drink in the past five years?"

My eyes go wide and they dart to Kayne. My palms sweat and my heart flutters with anxiety. A question, the first question he's asked me about the past five years. This is it. The first small step before he wants to know everything, all the gory details and then he's going to know what they did to me, what I was too weak to stop.

Kayne must notice me panic because he rounds my body and looks straight into my frightened eyes.

"What happened just then? What did I do?"

The woman places my drink in front of me and I pick it up quickly, I stare down at the ice floating in the drink and try to calm my racing heart. I glimpse up to Kayne 's face trying hard to hide the fear I have inside myself.

"Jesus, what is it Emmy?" It appears I failed.

"It's nothing. And no I haven't had alcohol since—" I stop mid-sentence, trying to remember when my last drink was, but I can't remember. "I can't remember when," I end softly.

"Baby, it's okay. You deserve to have some drinks and enjoy yourself. Just take it easy, okay. You don't want to be sleeping next to the toilet bowl tonight."

I nod, step away from him, and move among the people in the room to find my parents. I need space away from Kayne.

I find my parents and stand by my dad. In all this, he is the one person I know won't ask me the questions I never want to answer. My dad is a tower of strength, but I guess since everyone can see straight through me, I get that from him because I can see straight through him too. Every time he looks at me, I see his world turn dark. If I could change that I would. If I could tell him honestly that I'm okay, then I would, but I can't. I'm trying my hardest, but it's just not enough to save the ones I love around me and stop them from hurting.

I stand next to my parents for most of the night. A few hours later, I spot Kayne talking and laughing with a woman. My hand instantly reaches up and holds my rose necklace. I rub my thumb over the glass orb and my heart calms. Kayne must sense my stare because he looks up at me, then his eyes fall to my hand holding my rose petals. The woman continues to talk to him while he stares at me. She places her hand on his arm to grab his attention back and it works. He turns back to the woman and their laughs and chatter echo around me.

Suddenly, I feel warm. I place the back of my hand to my head and feel sweat there. I walk back over to the bar and order a tequila shot. I stopped drinking earlier and feel fine, but if I have to keep hearing the annoying, scratchy female laugh, then

I'm going to need more alcohol.

I down the shot, and then notice a familiar arm stretch out beside me and lean on the bar. Kayne 's warm, minty breath floats across my cheek as he says, "We need to talk, now. Privately."

Kayne pulls me by my elbow and we walk through the crowd and out of the function room. We're in a hallway and I think he's going to stop just here, but he continues down the hall and a set of stairs toward the front glass doors.

At the bottom of the stairs, Kayne turns us left and directs us into a room. It's dark, but the lights from the golf course shine into the room, illuminating it enough to be able to see clearly.

I hear the door close and turn to see Kayne watching me. His jaw is clenched and his posture is stiff.

"Fuck, you're good, you know that? Christ, some days I'm scared shitless that your words are true, that you really do want me to move on. But seeing that," he points to the room above us, "seeing you jealous, fuck, that feels good," he says with a frustrated laugh.

I stare at him with a blank expression. I'm exhausted. Lying, pretending, it's all so tiring.

"I saw you rubbing your necklace when you saw me talking to the woman. For one fucking second just admit it, Emmy. You want me as much as I want you. Stop pretending to be this person you're not, and for one moment, you might actually remember what it's like to be yourself, and not this woman who thinks she knows what's best for everyone else," he ends on a yell.

"Kayne, me touching my necklace means nothing. It's just a necklace. You can talk to whomever you want," I lie.

My necklace is everything to me. It represents who I was when I had a future. It's a time in my life when everything was perfect and it reminds me that at some point in my existence, Kayne and I had a future.

"Bullshit, Emily. I know you. Your necklace means a lot more to you than you're willing to reveal. Christ, just admit it!" Kayne shouts, frustration lacing his tone, but it's the desperation that breaks my heart.

Argh! I hate he knows me so well. I want to prove him wrong, just this once. I rip the necklace from my neck and hold it out to him.

"Take it then. It means nothing to me." I'm shaking. I'm not actually going to give it to him, I could never part with my rose.

Kayne jerks back as if I've just slapped him. Then quick as a flash it's ripped from my hand;

Kayne swings his arm back and my rose is thundering through the air straight at the wall. I don't even hear the clash that should come with glass smashing against a wall. I feel my knees hit the ground, but I just keep staring at the shattered glass and ripped petals on the floor.

Kayne rushes to the glass and starts picking up the shredded rose petals. "Fuck!" he bellows to the shattered glass. Look what my doubts and fears have done to him. He's on his knees picking up nine-year-old rose petals.

"Stop," I whisper. "You're right."

Kayne 's eyes dart to me and I watch as anguish crosses his features. He's ready for the rejection and that makes my heart splinter in two, once again seeing the pain I have put him through.

"You want the truth? Here it is. Yes, Kayne, I want you. I want you more than the dirt desires the rain. I *need* you. You give me reason to breathe, to live, to grow into the person I hope I can still be. I *hope* every day you can find the Emmy I used to be. I'm tired of running and turning away from you. I don't want to say goodbye to the only man I will ever love. I don't think I can live without you."

"You don't have to, Emmy. You will never have to say goodbye to me. Ever."

"But I do. All I do is hurt you. Don't you see,

you just left a party where you were laughing and having a good time with a *normal* woman. And where are you now Kayne? With me in a dark room, hurting. Begging a broken and unworthy woman to give you a chance."

"Stop!" he roars.

I shut my mouth shaking my head. He asks for the truth, yet he won't accept it.

Kayne stands up from the broken glass and shredded petals, and comes to me. He kneels in front of me, his expression soft, however his lips are tightly pressed together with his brows creasing from the determination in his eyes.. "Our life will be filled with smiles. We *will* be happy, Emmy. Even if it fucking kills me, we will be. These are our dark days, baby, but they won't last forever." His tone is full of desperation and pleading.

"This darkness lives within me. It's not going away, Kayne. If I let us happen, I'm committing you to the same horrible fate. A day doesn't go by that I don't want to scratch my skin raw to eradicate the *feeling* of those bastards on me. Do you want to see that for the rest of your life: the woman you love, struggling to breathe every day? Knowing you can't help her."

"I want whatever life you can give me, Emmy. You haven't even let me try to help you. How do you know that's not exactly what you need? I will

171

save you every time you want to die. I will pick you up every time I see a frown on your beautiful face. I will tell you how amazing you are, every day for the rest of my life, until my dying day. There is no beginning and no end without you. I believe the dark will pass."

I say the words I know will stop him from living in a fantasy world. "I won't have children, Kayne. "

"I will sacrifice that for you," Kayne speaks without missing a beat. His words are strained and his eyes go glassy.

A loud cry bursts from my mouth and it echoes all around the empty room. It bounces off the intense waves surrounding us as we fight for each other—me to let Kayne go, and Kayne to hold on to me.

"Can you see it now? That I will do whatever it takes to be with you."

I nod. "I'm scared I'm dooming you to my nightmare," I say through my sobs.

"I'm with you or I'm wasting my life away waiting for you. Just *try,* for me, Emmy, please."

Sobs rip from my chest as my walls crumble and my well-constructed defense waves its white flag and I finally let Kayne in.

Chapter Eighteen

Kayne picks me up off the floor, carries me to his car and drives us home. *Home.* I can say that now. Our home. Weight lifts off my shoulders as I decide to move forward in my life with Kayne by my side. No more fighting to save him. He's determined to go down with me. Maybe Lily's right. Maybe if we fight, together we can make it. We can come to a place in our life that's bearable. I don't think I'll ever be whole, but if I can just find the halfway mark, it might be enough to give Kayne the life he deserves.

On the ride home, he calls my dad to tell him we had to leave. We arrive home and Kayne comes around to my side. He takes my hand and walks me inside. We go straight to the bedroom and shower together. Nothing sexual, just the need to wipe away the day's heartache and comfort each other.

We dry ourselves and lay in bed, naked together in each other's arms. The difference between gentle touches and the harsh ones I have come to know reminds me of my past. Dark memories flitter around my mind, but I push them away. They don't belong here. I'm safe, loved and wanted.

My fingers have itched to touch Kayne ever since I came back. Now, he's in my arms, free to touch wherever I want. I slide my fingers into his hair and Kayne looks down at me at the same time. The yearning swirling in his gorgeous blue eyes gives me the permission I'm looking for.

Kayne glides his arms around my waist and pulls me up toward him. I kiss him. Immediately, he opens for me and my tongue slides into his mouth. I moan at tasting the delicious combination of Kayne and beer.

Kayne 's hand moves down my body and rests just above my clit. My heart speeds up. I'm desperate for him to touch it, to touch me.

Kayne 's head drops to my neck and in a rough voice he says, "Emmy, I want to touch every part of your body tonight. I want to caress your gorgeous ass. I want to cup and squeeze your beautiful tits and most of all I want to touch and taste your pussy, *my* pussy. If you don't want that, tell me and we can go slowly. Wait until you're ready. What do you want, baby?"

"Oh, my God," I breathe against Kayne 's ear.

"I need you so badly, Kayne. I want you to do all of those things to me, right now." I rub my sensitive clit against his thigh. My body is in hyper drive and it needs a release now.

"Jesus, Emmy, thank God. I need you so fucking badly right now." Kayne 's voice is even rougher this time when he speaks and is thick with relief.

His hand lowers and he cups my pussy, the whole thing with his large, warm calloused hand. He tightens his hand on my heat and growls into my neck. "*Mine.*"

I inhale sharply and my eyes go glassy.

Kayne leaves his hand cupping my pussy as he strokes my clit with his thumb. My body ignites at the first swirl of his finger. My nerve endings going off like fireworks.

Kayne pulls back from my neck and stares down into my eyes while I breathe out in ecstasy from his powerful but gentle strokes on my clit. It's not long before my hips buck and my orgasm builds fast.

"You like that, Emmy?" Kayne asks against my mouth as he kisses the corners of my lips and around my jaw.

I realize my fingers are still in his hair and grasp on tightly to his strands to show Kayne how much I'm liking what he's doing. He sucks my neck at the same time he speeds up his circles and strokes on my clit.

"Fuck, Emmy, you're so beautiful. I would never forget how stunning you look when I had my hands on you and when you're about to come, but my memory didn't do you justice."

I take in Kayne 's raspy, sexy words, but I can't respond. I can't do anything except feel the delicious sensation running up my legs and straight to my clit.

Kayne pulls his hand away and my head shoots up to find out why, but before the protest sitting on my lips escapes, Kayne 's mouth is on me and he is sucking and licking my clit. My hips buck once again from the amazing sensation. I grasp the bed sheets as the orgasm rebuilds.

"Kayne," I pant, my hips pushing my pussy as far into his mouth as they can. I whimper as the explosion is about to hit. My pussy contracts and pleasure slams into me as I scream out Kayne 's name.

I come out of my blissful fog and find Kayne grinning down at me. He sits back on his haunches and strokes his cock. I whimper at the sight. We used to touch ourselves in front of each other and get off on watching the other. Our sex life never lacked anything. Kayne and I were perfect for each other in so many ways.

"You ready for me to take you, Emmy?"

"Yes," I breathe out, unable to take my eyes from his hand stroking his hard cock.

"Do you want me to use a condom, baby?"

That question instantly pulls me from my sex-induced coma. Does he want to use a condom? We never did before. I was always on the pill. I've been on the pill for the past five years. It was the one thing I thanked God for. During the parties, the women had to be on the pill and the men had to wear condoms. Does Kayne think I'm dirty?

"Emmy," Kayne says my name ever so gently that my eyes swing to his instantly.

"I'm clean," I blurt out. "I went to the doctor remember, when I came back." I start moving from the bed; I'm retreating. My confidence has plummeted.

I don't move far before Kayne has his arm wrapped around my waist and he hauls me back to the bed on my back, hovering over me.

"Baby, I know. Jesus, I love you, Emmy, I wouldn't care if you went to a doctor, and I trust you. Going bareback with you is fucking heaven. I'm talking about what you said earlier. You don't want kids, which means we should probably be extra careful. What do you think?"

"Oh," is all that comes out. He's respecting my wishing about not wanting to have children. I've ruined the moment, the whole night. My stupid insecurities and doubts. "I'm so sorry. I've ruined the night." I turn my head to the side, unable to look at Kayne anymore. And then I hear him chuckle and my head swings back to see what he finds so funny. He's smiling at me and I narrow my eyes at him.

"Emmy, I've waited five fucking years to be inside your pussy again. You did not ruin anything over one sentence that can easily be forgotten because it's not important. Not as important as we are."

I nod slowly while my heart pounds against my chest. It's a good pound; it's my heart telling me he's amazing and I'm the luckiest woman in the world.

"I'll wear the condom tonight and we can talk about it more another time, okay?"

I nod again, unable to speak. I'm too focused on staring at this amazing man of mine. *Mine.*

Kayne positions himself between my legs. I wrap them around his waist. He grasps the base of his cock and positions it at my entrance. My breathing accelerates as I impatiently wait for him to push inside me.

He does, slowly and gently. I moan in pleasure as the glorious length of him fills me. He stops when he's all the way in and looks down at me. His eyes are asking me if I'm okay, but I'm frustrated. I want him to push me like he used to, not treat me like something that may break at any minute.

"Kayne, I need you to move. Don't treat me like glass. I'm not going to break. I want what we use to have; raw, beautiful fucking which always fell into lovemaking. I want that right now."

At my words, Kayne kisses me hard. My mouth opens and we devour each other. He thrusts in and out in blissful strokes. I moan into his mouth and Kayne pulls back, breathing heavily as he keeps pumping into me vigorously. Whimpers fall from my lips as another orgasm builds.

My eyes close as my legs begin to tremble, pleasure and heat attacks every inch of my body. "Yes," I breathe out. "Harder."

Kayne does as I ask and slams into me harder and faster. His growls spur my orgasm to breaking point.

"This is beautiful," I whisper.

"No, I'm looking at real beauty right now, baby."

I open my eyes to Kayne starting down at me. My fingers tighten their grip on his shoulders as the

179

wave of pleasure rolls through me. My back arches and I scream out in ecstasy.

As the waves slowly roll away, Kayne buries his face into my neck and growls against my sweat glistened skin as he thrusts in a few more times, then slows and stops. He bites my shoulder and then sucks the bite and kisses it.

"Mine," he states loudly. "My beautiful girl is home," he whispers the last part into my neck.

My heart swells and tears fall from my eyes. *I am home.*

I softly say what's been on the tip of my tongue since I've been home. I say the words I can never take back. There will be no turning around, no hiding away and no trying to save him from my dark and corrupted world. Now, we are in this together.

"I love you, Kayne. "

Chapter Nineteen

It's been a three weeks since I gave into Kayne. The first week was full of passionate sex and heated arguments. At times, I shut him out. I didn't mean to. It's just wired into me to deal with my own problems and process the nightmares on my own, and Kayne can easily see when some moments are a struggle for me.

Three days into our new relationship, the urge to cut was great. I found myself in the bathroom begging myself not to pick up the razor. I noticed Kayne come into my vision on the left and I tried to relax my body, looking around the bathroom pretending to search for something.

"Emmy, what's going on?" It's easy to hear his anxiety.

I cross my arms, rub my biceps and say, "Nothing, I'm just going to have a shower."

I extend my arm out and swing the bathroom

door closed but I hear a thump and then the door opens back up. Kayne stands there in the doorway, narrowing his eyes at me.

"Bullshit, Emmy, tell me what the fuck is going on? You looked like you were about to rip the fucking basin from its stand." His voice goes from anxiety to concern quickly.

"I just need a minute," I say softly.

"Fuck that. You promised you would try, Emmy. Tell me what's going on up in that beautiful head of yours."

I move back two steps and sit on the toilet lid.

"I'm just having a bad day, that's all," I say.

"I can see that, Emmy," Kayne states gently. "But you have to tell me when you have these moments, baby. I need to be here to help you. If not for you, then do it for me, Emily. It kills me to think of you going through this on your own." Kayne's voice is thick with emotion and the sound tears at my heart.

I nod slowly. Anxious at speaking the words that have been locked up in my mind for so long. Every night in the dark, Kayne has asked me to tell him something about the last five years. I've kept it to mostly how I felt during those times and not what was actually done to me. But the nightmare from last night and the memories swirling in my mind right now are far from what I want Kayne to know about me. Something I never want him ever to have to visualize.

"Tell me, baby. Tell me so you can get it out."

I look up to Kayne. My vision blurs from my glassy eyes, but I hold strong and don't let any fall.

"I love you," I say with trembling lips.

Kayne cups my cheeks with his warms hands and says, "I know you do, Emmy, and I love you more than anything in this world."

I take a big breath in and my lip quivers. "Then you need to understand I can't share it all with you. I don't want you knowing it all, Kayne. I don't want these memories or thoughts in your head." I tap his temple. "I want to share with you how I felt, how I dealt with it. But I need you to trust me when I say telling you what was done to me, won't help me move on. It will only hurt us both." I look into his eyes and observe as he processes my words.

"I understand, Emmy. I don't know what I'm doing here. I just want to help you, and if that is the best way to help you, then consider it done. I'll listen to you and not push for more."

I let out a huge breath.

"Thank you," I softly say before kissing him. We end the kiss and I see the question in his eyes; am I okay? Has the moment passed?

183

"I had a nightmare last night. They aren't nightmares which have me waking up in a fright. I just wake up in the morning and those memories associated with the bad dream are the first thing I think of and they stick with me throughout the day."

Unwelcome tears fall down my cheeks as I explain to Kayne the feelings these memories evoke in me.

"The thought of being left to the dark all on my own… the belief of being deserted… the knowledge that no one is listening… desperation to give up… it's all so familiar and I know how easy it is to go numb. It's much more bearable than feeling the pain."

I dash my tears away roughly. "I lie to myself too easily. Telling myself I was coming to our room to stop myself from cutting. Yet I ended up in the one place I knew where the razors were. I'm desperate to clear my mind of these memories and cutting does that for me. But remembering the hurt on your face when you saw how far I had gone, that stops me every time. Still, I want to learn to stop for myself, not for someone else."

"Emily, you saying this shows how far you have come. I want you to do this for you, too. Not for me, for the strong Emily I know is right here." He places his flat palm over my heart.

My lips tremble as tears continue to fall. "I'm trying so damn hard. I promise, I am."

"Oh, baby, I know it. I watch my strong Emmy re-emerge a little more every day."

I peer up at Kayne in shock. Can he? Sometimes I catch myself doing or saying something the old Emmy would have done, but I'm scared to believe it's happening; that I'm actually healing. But he can see her? Hope surges through me like wildfire.

The end of week one, was also when I smiled for the first time in five years. That's right. I did it. I smiled. And while I remember the moment, tears pool in my eyes because I didn't just smile; I did a hell of a lot more.

I'm upstairs sorting through my pictures I took last night. Kayne took me out to dinner, our first date in five years. Afterwards, we went for a walk through town. I grabbed my camera from the car and spotted many couples holding hands, smiling, laughing and kissing. I snapped any pictures. Kayne didn't mind. He actually helped me spot the exact moment on someone's face he knew I was looking for. That sincere expression when you know the person is thinking how lucky they are, how perfect their life is for that one precious moment.

So I'm in my bedroom sorting my pictures because Kayne asked me to stay upstairs for the morning. He said he had a surprise for me. I have no idea what it could be and I'm desperate to look out our bedroom window because I can hear him moving around the outside of the house. However, I stop myself, continue sorting pictures and decide which ones I will print to have downstairs.

"Emmy! You can come down now!"

Straight away I jump from the bed and race down the stairs. My heart's pounding in rhythm with my excitement. I reach the bottom of the stairs and watch Kayne say goodbye to Jake, Dom & Nick through the open front door. I didn't even realize they were here.

Kayne jogs from the front into the house, a huge grin on his face. I see the sweat of hard work on his white t-shirt and what looks like dirt on his black board shorts.

"What were they doing here?"

"You'll see," he says with a wink.

My confusion must show on my face because Kayne laughs out loud and says, "Come on, Emmy. Time to take you out of the dark."

His gaze on me intensifies and I sense his words mean more than just to let me in on the secret.

Kayne reaches out for me and I see and feel the specks of dirt on his hand as I take his fingers and entwine them with mine. What the heck? He's covered in dirt?

He walks me through the dining room, past all my pictures through the kitchen and straight to the back door.

Before opening the door, he turns to me and says, "Close your eyes, Emmy."

I furrow my brow and try to look around him, but he moves to the side and blocks my view.

"Nuh uh, close those beautiful brown eyes, baby, now." His voice is sweet but firm.

I bite my bottom lip, cross my arms over my chest and close my eyes tightly.

Kayne's hands grasp my shoulders and then I sense his face move to me. He's so close I can smell his aftershave. Then his warm lips are kissing my neck, up to my ear.

"Emmy, you cross your arms and push those beautiful tits up, and how am I supposed concentrate on leading you anywhere."

Kayne's kisses move down and across my jaw and I melt into his body with a sigh.

I love his hands and mouth on me, so tender and loving. Heat spreads between my legs just as Kayne pulls away and I let out a whimper in protest.

Kayne chuckles. "Later, baby, I promise. Now keep your eyes closed," he whispers against my cheek before kissing each of my eyelids softly.

Kayne gently pulls me through the backdoor. I visualize my backyard.

A large white fence that goes around our half-an-acre of beautiful, green grass. Our garden shed in the left back corner of the yard, and I can imagine each and everyone one of our five tall trees that give great shade in the afternoons.

A cool breeze hits my legs and arms. Wearing only denim shorts and a black tank top, goose bumps form from the gust of wind.

My feet leave the cemented pergola area to the cool grass. I love the feeling of soft just-cut grass between my toes.

My lips tip up and for the first time in what feels like forever, I feel it and release a small smile. It doesn't disappear as soon as I notice it because I'm distracted by hearing birds.

I tip my head up as if to see them, but I just want to hear them once more. While doing that my ponytail blows in the wind, the breeze caressing my neck.

We walk into what I sense is the middle of the yard. I scrunch my face together when I think I can hear water.

"Kayne, did you buy me a pool?" I ask sarcastically.

"Not quite, Emmy. You can open your eyes now."

I do, slowly at first, but when all the pink and red colors hit my eyes, they fly open immediately.

I gasp. My hand covers my mouth in surprise and tears cascade down my face. I take a step back and just stare. I gaze at the most beautiful rose garden I have ever seen. A rose garden in my back yard.

Four circles are filled with pink and red roses, and in between those four circles are four white pebbled trails which meet up in the middle to a gorgeous water fountain with birds surrounding it. It's the most beautiful thing I have ever seen.

I move my hand away from my mouth and step to the roses closest to me. I touch a rose and feel the silkiness of the beautiful petals, just like my rose.

"Emmy, I wanted to give you something that was as beautiful as you are and something which would always remind you of us."

I tear my eyes from the roses to Kayne with what I imagine is shock and awe on my face.

Tears continue to fall as I speak, "In this moment, right now, I can think about that horrible time and all I can imagine is what I had to look forward to. This," I extend my arms out, "and you." I point to Kayne. "Every time you make love to me, every time you listen to me, every time you do something like this…" I trail off on a whisper, unable to continue through my clogged throat.

I clear my throat and speak more clearly this time. "I realize I was never alone. I know now why I chose to survive and not give up. Because you were always with me and I was never abandoned."

A cry escapes from my mouth as I say, "I don't know what to say, how to thank you for never giving up on me. You keep giving me hope and beauty in my dark world. You're lighting it up. What used to be a small light in a corner is now so bright, it fends off the monsters all on its own."

Kayne gives me a grand smile and it shows off his glassy eyes. "Love means never being alone, Emmy. If there is one thing in this world that is true and everlasting, it's my love for you, and that means you were, and will never be alone." Kayne reaches out to me and pulls me to him in an earth-shattering, passion-filled kiss. We detach breathing heavily and staring into each other's eyes.

Kayne grins and says, "Wanna fuck in the rose garden?"

And that's when it happened. The moment my whole life changed.

A loud laugh breaks from my mouth and releases into the world.

Kayne's eyes widen and his smile grows impossibly big as he laughs with me, but his is one of disbelief.

"Emmy!" he shouts, surprised by my laugh and smile.

I remain smiling, watching him as he stares at the outline of my mouth as if studying the curves and memorizing my smile.

I pounce on him and grab the collar of his shirt, wrapping my legs around his waist, I kiss him hard and long.

Kayne bends at the knees and we fall to the soft green grass right next to my beautiful roses and we make love, smiling and laughing almost the whole way through.

Week two was bliss. I smiled and laughed every day. It was like opening a box you could never close again. I never wanted to close the box, but I thought my smiles would come back low, far and few between. However, once I realized I could give Kayne so much more than I thought I was capable of, everything made me happy, made me smile.

Color fills my world once again. I have a dark side, but the light in my mind is conquering the dark. Now the monsters fear my once small bright light. The dark still tries to invade, but Kayne does or says something, touches, kisses, holds or makes love to me, and the dark doesn't stand a chance. Kayne *is* my bright light. He was always there in my mind; that small light, always fighting for me, even when I didn't realize it.

I roll my head to the side and take in a smiling Kayne staring at me while he breathes heavily. Yep, it's been a rocky three weeks, but it's also been the best three weeks of my life.

***

Kayne

Breathing heavily, Emily is sweaty and stunning. She grins at me and it's like an electric shock to my heart. I will never tire of her beautiful smile. I will never take her gorgeous, curved-up lips for granted. Sometimes I need to pinch myself to remember this is real; my Emmy is here. She's smiling and she's happy.

She's still staring at me as I reach over and pull her up by under her arms. I sit her on my waist, her ass cheeks resting on my softening cock. Emmy shakes her hips on my cock and smiles a devious grin at me.

I groan, growing hard again. I'm exhausted from our morning activities already.

"Baby, give a man five minutes in between fucking. That one was… Jesus Christ, that time was amazing, but I need food for energy before I can go again."

Emily laughs in response.

I reach to the side table and pick up my phone. I find the camera icon on the home screen, press video, and start filming the most beautiful woman in the world. *My Emmy.*

"Do that again," I ask Emmy.

She looks at me in confusion, and then gasps, saying excitedly, "You want to film me while I ride you?"

It wouldn't be the first time we've filmed ourselves during sex. Emmy and I went through a phase of that in our early twenties.

I laugh loudly at her guess and say, "No, baby, smiling, laughing, don't stop."

I have this sudden urge to record her smile and laugh. I went without it for five years. Now I don't even want to go a day. I need to film her so I can watch it whenever I want to. Need to, to remind myself this isn't a dream.

She continues to smile, but she seems to do it out of confusion and thinking I may have lost my mind.

All of sudden, Emmy stops smiling and licks her lips seductively.

My eyes shoot from the phone to her lips. She

begins to move down my body and past my waist. She lays soft kisses all over my dick. Emmy places my now painfully hard cock in her mouth and I can't hold back the groan.

"Christ." My voice comes out strangled.

I drop the phone to the bed, clasp Emmy's hair, and lay my head back, groaning in pleasure.

After long moments of Emmy torturing me with her hot, wet mouth, I reach down, lift her up, and place her over my thighs. She balances on her knees as I place the head of my cock at her entrance.

I rub the head of my cock back and forth through her dripping pussy. *Fuck.* Before I let her sink down around me, I lock my eyes to hers and cup one side of her face.

"I love you, Emmy."

With our gazes still locked, we both slam together at the same time. We shout out in ecstasy as our bodies join in an explosive way.

We grab hold of each other's hands, entwining our fingers together. Emmy pushes hard against my arms as she rises and slams back down onto me. It's brutal, hot, and fucking amazing.

The room is filled with Emmy's whimpers and my grunts. Fuck, there is nothing in this world like my cock encased in Emmy's warm, slick pussy. *Heaven.*

Her bouncing tits have me tearing my eyes away from her face. I push back on her arms, sit up halfway and take one of her nipples into my mouth. Delicious, soft, smooth, and fucking exquisite.

I moan against her breast as Emmy continues to ride me with her tight vise of a pussy. Fuck, I love being inside her. I never want this to end.

Emmy moans loudly and her walls blissfully contract and squeeze around my cock. Her movement becomes frenzied. She releases my hands and grasps my shoulders.

I take over, driving up into her hard, my cock begging for more of her. I want to go deeper, move closer. I want to crawl up inside her.

Her whimpers turn into screams of ecstasy. Her breathy, "Please, don't stop," has my balls growing tight and I know I'm close. Then it happens; I'm coming with her. My whole body vibrates and shakes as I explode deep within my girl, coating her insides with my cum.

Mine.

I fall back to the bed and Emmy lands on my sweaty chest. The only sounds in the room are our powerful breaths. I move her hair away and kiss her temple.

"Fuck, baby, you are going to kill me, you know that," I say with a chuckle.

Emmy laughs into my chest and the vibration of her giggle travels straight to my heart. It double beats with pride. Emily owns me body and soul. God, I love her so fucking much.

Emmy's tummy growls so I decide it's time to feed my girl. I slap her ass and whisper into her hair, "Off, baby, I'm going to shower, then make us something to eat."

Emily turns her head and stares up at me while leaning on my chest. Her face is flushed pink and her eyes sparkle with mischief.

"I already ate. I'm full," she says with a wink.

A laugh erupts from my mouth as Emmy hops off me. She lies on the bed beside me. I give her a hard closed-mouth kiss and then I jump off the bed and head straight into the shower.

I make it to the door and turn back to Emmy. She's facing the other way. My eyes roam over her naked back and her firm ass. My dick actually fucking stirs a little at that. I look down at it and think, *holy fucking shit, again, really?*

I turn around and walk into the shower laughing. Fuck yes! This is how every day is going to start for us from now on.

Chapter Twenty

Facing the window, listening to Kayne laugh as he gets in the shower, I can't help but hope every day starts like this.

Another smile graces my lips, one I'm very familiar with now, the sated, just-fucked, the happiest-I've-ever-been, I'm-home smile. I sigh. Life is close to perfect for us right now. My nightmares and memories are coming less and less every day. Lily was right. Letting Kayne in was all I needed all along. I was never going to be able to walk this road alone. It was always meant for Kayne and me, but life is only close to being perfect because there is one thing that weighs heavily on me: Donovan is still looking for me.

I've checked the laptop every day yet there are no updates from my informant. That means Donovan is still in New York and still looking for me. Each morning as Kayne goes downstairs to make breakfast, I pull the laptop out, and I'm afraid to open my emails. Not afraid Donovan could be coming for me. No, I know what I will do if we come face to face again. I *will* try to kill him.

What I'm afraid of is what will happen if Donovan captures me and kills me. Not for myself, but for Kayne. I know Kayne would never survive losing me again.

I've thought about telling him, telling Jake, have them take over and take Donovan out for me, but the revenge deep inside of me prevents me from speaking out. It wants to watch Donovan die. I want to watch him suffer. I'm trying hard to let that part of me go. I know being here for Kayne is more important.

Hearing water turn off in the shower jolts me from my thoughts and I roll over and watch a naked Kayne step out of the shower, dry himself off and walk to the closet, still naked. His firm ass sways as he moves. He's perfect. Every muscle on his body is taut and tight. He's a machine of muscle and God help Donovan if Kayne ever gets his hands on him. Actually, no, God would never help such an evil monster. Kayne throws on some basketball shorts, and then comes to my side of the bed to kiss me. Drops of water drip on my face from his wet hair.

"Shower, baby, and come down. I could hear your tummy rumbling from inside the shower," he says with a grin.

He couldn't have, but yes, I am starving. I smile and nod. Then he's up and walking out of the room.

I listen as his heavy footsteps leave the stairs, and when I know he's in the kitchen, I bounce out of bed and throw on my robe. I grab the laptop from my closet, where I've been hiding it the last few days. I sit on the bed and open it up. Then I see it. An unopened email. Opening it, the words *close* and *soon* jump out at me.

I've been able to get my hands on your file at the investigators. Donovan has found your school records. He's close to finding you. Soon he will know where you are.

Are you going to him like we planned? We need to move soon before he finds out where you live.

My heart squeezes and twists. *School records. Going to him.* I know I should go straight downstairs and tell Kayne this, but I'm still undecided, and I know I need to make a decision today.

I will get back to you soon with my plans.

I shut the laptop lid down and stare into thin air. Thoughts of finding Donovan, surprising him, kidnapping and hurting him run rampant through my mind. The temptation of revenge is so strong, but I'm not a fool. He would easily be twice as strong as me. I need a really good plan to make it work, an iron-tight strategy to make sure Kayne doesn't lose me again. God, this is foolish, taking any chances at all is stupid and not right. However, retribution flows through my blood, it's so hard to let go. My soul screams at me to jump on a plane and head to New York to show Donovan he has no power over me; that he never did.

"Emmy! Breakfast is almost ready. Five minutes!"

Kayne 's yell startles me. I jump from the bed and quickly head into the shower. I swiftly wash my body, dry myself, and choose a pair of jeans and a deep blue blouse. Then I'm racing down the stairs to the love of my life.

Kayne turns and gives me a blinding smile. He's so happy. Fear grips my heart imagining him standing in this kitchen alone, living in this house all by himself if something does happen to me. I can't let that happen.

"Your mom called while you were in the shower. She wants you to go shopping with her and Lily today."

"Oh, okay, sounds like fun."

It's Saturday and Mom likes to see me on Saturdays or Sundays. My parents try not to crowd me, but they are pushy to see me at least once on the weekends, which I understand.

I set the table for breakfast and we sit and start eating.

"What are you up to today?" I ask Kayne with a mouthful of bacon.

"Jake texted, said he's going to come round to watch the Colts game."

"Ooh, sounds like fun," I say sarcastically with a grin.

Kayne grins back at me. "Yeah, damn it, I'm going to miss looking in a hundred different shops and listening to girls squeal over material. I'm so disappointed I can't come." He ends with a wink and a grin.

I burst out laughing; my tummy muscles hurt from laughing so much already today. They aren't used to it.

After breakfast, we clean up and end up on the couch making out when we hear a knock on the front door.

For a brief moment, my heart somersaults at the thought it could be Donovan. I freeze on the spot as I watch Kayne open the front door and I don't relax until I see my mother walk in and give Kayne a hug. She smiles brightly over to me.

Looking at the smiling faces around me, I know I need to make a decision. I can't let this go for any longer. It's not safe. I promise myself to have a decision made by the time I get back from shopping. I already know which way I'm leaning, and that's to tell Kayne, have him deal with Donovan and then I can know that the man will be six feet underground soon.

But what if I need to watch Donovan suffer. Does my soul need that in order to fully recover? Or is it just the revenge I crave that's tempting me to be the last person he sees before he leaves this world.

***

Kayne

Jake and I watch as Barb drives off with both our girls. We stare at where the car drove off from only a few minutes ago.

Jake turns to me and pats me on the shoulder.

"A few hours and they'll be back. You got beers in the fridge?"

I look to Jake and nod. "Yeah, grab me one as well."

I glance back to the road one more time before heading inside with Jake.

My heart beats frantically at being away from Emmy. I've spent the last five years doing everything in my power to find her. It's hard to watch her leave my side.

Emmy doesn't know, but I know a lot more about her and the collection than she thinks I do. I dealt with scum to find locations for the collection and even killed men who laughed in my face when they told me they'd seen Emily and had a piece of her.

I know what happened to her. I have an idea about how many times she was raped. It kills me. Every day I wake up and remember what my girl has been through.

I knew almost every single thing about the collection and what happened to the women. The one thing I couldn't fucking find out was where they were keeping them housed between parties. Plus, the Intel on the parties was always too late; we'd turn up and the place would be empty. So many times I prepared myself to find her and then nothing. No one was there. My heart died a thousand deaths when I realized once again we were too late. Knowing what she must have gone through the night before shattered me to the core.

When Jake informed me we were finally going to find her, I was a wreck. I couldn't wait to have her in my arms, yet I was petrified by what I may find. What I did find was my girl, broken in her mind and soul. However, she was still my Emmy. She just needed time, and thank fuck, things are finally starting to get better, back to normal. She's smiling. She's laughing. Yeah, things are getting a hell of a lot better.

I walk inside, take a seat on the sofa and accept my beer from Jake. The game is starting and I try to focus, but my mind is still on Emmy. I pray she's safe. I can't ever lose her again. What are the chances of that ever happening another time? Probably one in a million, but those were the chances in the first place.

I've made sure no one from that fucking empire can hurt Emmy again. Jake and I both have been making sure of that for the last few months. We've been working with Joseph to track down the men who attended the parties. We've been taking them all out one by one.

Nick and Joseph have been the ones pulling the triggers while Jake and I stayed with our girls, but we know everything that happens. We know who's next and when. I take those moments and savor the seconds before I know a bullet will go through a man's heart. That he can never hurt another woman; can never hurt my Emmy again.

There's only one motherfucker who we are yet to track down. Donovan Bradley, a lawyer from Los Angeles, mid-thirties, always wears expensive suits and my Intel was that this fucker thought he owned Emily. I want to deal with him myself.

"Kayne, what the fuck are you thinking about that has you grinding your teeth together like fucking steel? It's louder than the damn TV."

I turn to Jake with hard eyes. "You heard from Joseph or Nick yet?"

Jake sighs. "No, they're still looking for the fucker. They lost him in Mexico City. Joseph said he has two guys missing. One who last reported Donovan in Florida and one who followed him to Mexico City. Both of his guys haven't been heard from since. Joseph is pissed. He has no leads on where Alexa is and his guys keep disappearing. Every time I've spoken to him, he sounds like he's ready to kill. I think the only thing that has kept him sane the last few months has been killing these fucking assholes."

Jake sits forward and sighs, "Lil asked me a about a phone conversation she overheard. I was asking Nick if the job was done. She asked me straight out, as only Lil ever does, no bullshit. I was honest with her. She knows what we're doing. She told me she doesn't want to know anymore and she understands. She fucking grinned and gave me the best blow job I've ever had after that. My woman is fucking feisty and amazing," Jake finishes with a massive smile on his face.

I can't help but smile myself. Lily is feisty, a woman who's lost so much and yet she has so much fight left in her. Her pictures are the ones Emily used to stare at the most. I know Emily idolizes Lily, but Emmy doesn't see she's just as much a fighter if not more than Lily. My girl's a survivor 'til the end.

"I was going to give Joseph a call today while I was here, get an update. I'll do it now."

I nod to Jake and he grabs his phone from his back pocket. He presses some keys before turning the speakerphone on and we hear the ringing tone.

"Jake, fuck, I was just about to call you!" Joseph answers, yelling into the phone.

There's a loud roar of an engine and strong winds in the background.

"Where the hell are you, Joseph?" Jake asks.

"Just getting off my jet at Hasting Airport. Things have changed and I needed to come to you guys. We need to meet. Where can I find you?"

I look up to Jake, shocked by Joseph's words.

Jake gives Joseph my home address and they hang up.

We're both left surprised and wondering what's changed so much that Joseph O'Connor needs to see us in person.

YOU LOVED ME AT MY WEAKIEST

Chapter Twenty One

An anxious hour later, a black sedan pulls up my driveway. I've only seen Joseph in photos before. When we first started searching for Emily, he was on the top of our list to follow, but he ended up being an ally instead of an enemy and he continues to prove he's nothing like his monster of a father.

A tall, broad shouldered man with black hair and a five o'clock shadow climbs out of the car. His face is hard and his eyes determined. That's what always caught my attention about Joseph in his pictures; his face always showed his harsh upbringing and corrupt life. He looked perpetually angry.

Except the pictures I took of him with Alexa Kingsley; they were the only times I saw him even remotely happy and he looked at her as if she was his whole life. He would do anything for that woman. I don't know why she ran from him, but I do know he has dozens of men all over the world looking for her. He's been helping Jake and me, but when he gets leads on Alexia, he drops our mission straight away to follow up and see if he's finally found her. We understand. It's frustrating that these men don't die sooner, but we understand; he needs her, just like I need Emmy and Jake needs Lily. They are ours and we are theirs. There is no one else for us.

Joseph walks up the porch steps and moves toward Jake. They shake hands and pat each other on the shoulder.

Joseph turns to me and we shake hands. He looks me right in the face, his expression showing sincere remorse. Remorse for everything I've been through or maybe what he knows Emily went through. I tighten my jaw. I'm angry. I know none of this is his fault, but he stood by and let so many bad things happen. I understand how powerful his father was, but when it comes to Emmy, common sense leaves me and all I care about is that she needed to be saved right from the start.

I squeeze his hand hard, brutally hard. I see him flinch, but he never tries to pull back. He just keeps the same regretful expression.

"Kayne," Jake says with a warning tone.

I release Joseph's hand and try to shake off my

dark thoughts.

"It's cool. I get it, but we need to move on. Some bad shit is coming your way, and soon," Joseph states.

We give each other a chin lift and walk inside the house, but before Jake and I move to the living room, Joseph starts talking and what he says stops us in our tracks. "Donovan Bradley is looking for Emily."

Jake and I freeze on the spot. I don't know about Jake, but at that moment, my blood runs cold and fear grips my heart.

I'm going to kill the bastard.

"Where is he?" I growl, my jaw ticking and my hands turning into fists. My anger is palpable.

"We found him again, this time in New York. I had another guy on him and now he is MIA as well," Joseph growls. "When I get my hands on the fucking person messing with my guys, they are gonna wish they were never born," Joseph grinds out.

"Get to the point," I say, my tone taut.

"Before my guy went missing, he reported back that Donovan was meeting a man called Bruce Stephens. Stephens is an investigator, and after some digging, we discovered he is looking for an Emily Roberts. Now, my guy's next instructions were to follow Donovan and send me the address he's staying at. I received an email from him, but for some fucking reason, the email I have is encrypted and now I can't get a hold of my guy."

"Well, how the fuck do we find out where he is now then?" I shout angrily at Joseph. He doesn't even blink at me.

"Kayne, fuck, calm the hell down. Yelling at each other isn't going to find the bastard any sooner. We need a plan," Jake states.

I know he's right, but all I can see is red. I want to smash something. I need that bastard in front of me so I can rip his insides out with my bare hands.

We're standing at the bottom of the stairs right next to the front door and it suddenly hits me, in a few hours, Emmy is going to come through the front door and I'm going to have to tell her the monster from her past, one of them, is looking for her. She's come so far; I'm afraid this could set her back. I want to protect her and deal with it without her knowing, but I know I need to be honest with her.

"I understand your frustration. Trust me, I do," Joseph growls out. "Someone is messing with me and my guys and I can't fucking find a single clue on who it is," Joseph shouts and his hands fly up into the air in frustration. "To know the email was coming to me and to encrypt it, that shit isn't easy. They would have had to have access to my system to encrypt that one and only message. They didn't touch anything else, didn't steal any other information from me. This doesn't make any sense, but someone definitely doesn't want me to find Donovan.

Desperation courses through my body. I feel as if someone is choking me. I need control over this situation. There are too many what ifs, too many roadblocks and possibilities I may lose Emily again. I turn my back to the guys and clench my hands. I want to smash something. I need to expel some of this rage. Joseph gets my attention again with his next words.

"I can still find out where Donovan is. My guys know to send another message with the information to another email address off the grid. It's in case of emergencies like this, but I can't use my internet provider or devices just in case. I'm gonna need to use someone else's computer to do it. This is half the reason why I'm here."

Half the reason, there's more? *Fucking great.*

"What else is it, Joseph?" Jake asks, not wanting to wait any longer for the information.

"My uncle, Michael O'Connor, I contacted him when I found out Donovan paid him a visit. I asked him what he wanted. He was vague and only said he was looking for someone and didn't say who. I didn't push the subject. Trust me, you don't push my uncle; he's one-step up from my father in the crazy department. He brought up finding out who killed my dad. He's trying to find out what happened, but can't seem to find anyone still alive to tell him. He also invited me to come and stay with him, and trust me, it's an invitation I can't ignore. He's suspicious I'm alive and everyone else is dead. He asked about the collection pieces and finding them again, to continue where Marco left off."

The air goes from calm to nuclear in about two seconds flat. Joseph steps back from Jake and me, and I can only imagine what he's seeing. Two murderous glares from men who are about to explode.

"Fuck, I know. I know!" Joseph shouts, his voice strong, but the sliver of fear is there.

"The two of you need to calm down. I told him everyone died, everyone, including the collection pieces and the slaves. I fucking had no idea what else to say. I told him the government came through with no warrants and no authority and took everyone out, including the girls so there were no witnesses. I told him it was over the money and the politicians my father was blackmailing. I also told him I received a heads up about it and disappeared before it happened, but my father was at the secret location so I couldn't warn him. My uncle knows my father never told anyone where the house was. For now, I think he believes me, but if Donovan finds Emily and is able to tell my uncle she's alive, then my uncle is going to know I lied, then my mother's life is on the line, as is mine. Not to mention Lexi. He knows how much she means to me." Joseph blows out a big breath.

"Do you think your uncle could find Alexa if you haven't been able to?" Jake asks Joseph.

Joseph grunts out a laugh. "I don't think so, but fuck, I'd love to have him try; then I might actually fucking find her. Lexi has always been good at this shit. Growing up around her fucked-up family and around mine, she's learned a lot."

There's so much pressure in my head. I grab my head and shake it, unable to comprehend Joseph's words. Marco's brother, a man apparently worse than the sick fuck Marco, is alive and wanting to startup the collection. The bastard needs to die and soon.

"We need to deal with your uncle. I won't leave any loose ends when it comes to Lily and Emily's safety." Jake states.

"Yeah, well, it's not going to be easy to kill him. If it was, I would have done it already. He's important to the drug and gun trade in Mexico. I'm going to visit him like he wants and work out where he's going with all this and what information he has. If we have to take him out, I need to make it look like an outside job from an enemy." Joseph stops talking and there's no flicker of emotion at killing his uncle, just sheer determination and knowledge that it will be the right thing to do.

"We'll deal with your uncle after Donovan. I can't focus on anything until motherfucking Donovan is dead," I grind out.

"Okay then, boys, we need a plan, and I need to bring Dom and Nick in on this. I have a laptop at my house. Let's head over now," Jake states while pulling his phone to his ear. "I'll call Mom and tell her to drop the girls at my place."

Jake starts for the door but I stop him. "Wait. I don't want Emmy to worry while she's out shopping. They'll know something is up. Emily has a laptop upstairs and we have Wi-Fi here. We'll figure out a plan here first so we have something to tell the girls before they can worry about anything."

Jake nods in understanding and we all move into the living area, Jake with his phone to his ear.

"Dom, head to Kayne 's place. We need to meet." Then he dials again and says the same thing, but this time to Nick.

I bend down to pull the laptop out from under

the coffee table, but it's not there. I race up the stairs two at a time and enter our bedroom. I've seen Emmy with the laptop up here looking over pictures plenty of times. Maybe she never took it back downstairs. My eyes search the room and I find the laptop on our bed, among the scatter covers. Emmy must have used it this morning.

I take the laptop downstairs to the dining table, carefully moving her pictures over. They are still on our table and around our dining room. Emmy has put some away, mostly the ones of strangers but she's kept out the ones of our friends and family and some she's snapped of the two of us together. I have a surprise planned for Emmy in the next few weeks. Tomorrow, I have a meeting with a construction company to talk about building onto our house. I'm going to build Emmy a photography studio. Emmy only sees the smiles and laugh lines on these people's faces, but what I see is art; she takes beautiful pictures. She changes the settings on the camera and a dark, stormy day becomes a vibrant, picture that comes alive with her changes. She thinks she's just highlighting their smiles, laughter and happy moments, but I don't think she realizes it's her who makes the pictures shine. I lift the laptop lid and see it's open to an email account.

I lift the laptop lid and see it's open to an email account.

"What the fuck?" I whisper, unable to believe what I'm reading—not wanting to believe it.

Both Jake and Joseph come up behind me and read over my shoulder.

From: A. Kingsley

Subject: I found him.

To: Emily Roberts

I'm in Mexico City. The man he's with is Marco's brother Michael O'Connor. He's been asking questions about what happened to his brother and there are rumors he's set to start off where Marco's empire died.

From my Intel, I've found out Donovan has arranged this meeting with Michael in hopes of finding you.

From: Emily Roberts

Subject: I found him.

To: A. Kingsley

I need you to keep him in your sights. I need to know where he is at all times. When I figure out what my plans are I will contact you through this email.

From: A. Kingsley

Subject: I found him.

To: Emily Roberts

Consider it done. Will I be seeing you soon?

From: Emily Roberts

Subject: I found him.

To: A. Kingsley

As soon as I can get out of Hastings, I will be there.

From: A. Kingsley

Subject: He's on the move.

To: Emily Roberts

Donovan is on his way to the USA. He boarded a flight to New York. I'm on the same flight. He hired an investigator to find you. The investigator is in New York City. He has nothing on you yet, but he's good. It will only be a matter of time before he finds you.

From: A. Kingsley

Subject: He's close.

To: Emily Roberts

I've been able to get my hands on your file at the investigators. Donovan has found your school records. He's close to finding you. Soon he will know where you are.

Are you coming to him like we planned? We need to move soon before he finds out where you live.

From: Emily Roberts

Subject: He's close.

To: A. Kingsley

I will get back to you soon with my plans.

My whole body seizes with panic and vibrates, with what I don't know, anger, betrayal, astonishment that Emily is this stupid and would actually try going up against a man like this.

Bile rises up my throat and threatens to empty as I think of the possibilities which could have happened if she left to find Donovan, and do what? My guess is she wants revenge and I can understand that, even cheer her on, but fuck, not to do it on her own. Honestly, not to do at all. If I have my way, she's not getting anywhere near the motherfucker.

I can't believe she would take this risk with her life and leave me, possibly leave me forever this time. I'm furious, and hurt. How little do I mean to her if she would risk putting me through this again?

Joseph practically rips the laptop from my hands, but I'm too stunned to care.

"Lexi," I hear him whisper. "Alexa has been helping Emily find Donovan. She's been trailing him." Joseph's voice is low and angry.

"Fuck, Em, what are you doing!" Jake shouts. "And Alexia, she's been the one messing with your guys?" Jake asks just as surprised as Joseph and me.

"Well, fuck, at least I know they are still alive. I just need to find where she's fucking hog tied and left them," Joseph says, exasperated.

"She's been fucking trailing a serial rapist, by herself!" he roars into the room.

Jake and I both step back from him the growing anger pouring out of him in waves. I glance around the room thinking of what to try and save if he goes to smash something. I know if I found out Emily was actually following around a man like Donovan, I would lose my shit.

Instead, Joseph places the laptop down on the table, takes a seat in the chair and starts typing.

Jake and I both stand behind him and watch as he writes.

From: Emily Roberts

Subject: I found YOU.

To: A. Kingsley

Wait till I get my hands on you Lexi, your ass is gonna be red raw. Get the fuck off that sicko's trail and tell me where you are, NOW!

Joey

While Joseph death stares the laptop waiting for Alexa to reply, Jake and I walk into the entry.

"My hands are fucking shaking, Jake. That's how angry I am with Emmy right now."

"I know my little sister is in deep shit right now. She has no idea the storm waiting for her when she gets home."

"I can't even think. I'm so pissed at her. We just got her back and she was going to run off and come face to face with that fucker. Possibly never come home this time. FUCK!" I shout to the roof.

I hear Joseph on the phone talking to someone about tracing an email address when I hear a car pull in.

I peer out the window and find Nick and Dom getting out of the car. Time to plan, time to decide how and when Donovan Bradley will die, painfully.

Chapter Twenty-Two

We pull into my driveway laughing as my mom tells Lily about Jake's teenage years and his squeaky voice.

"He wouldn't leave the house for months," she says, while trying to control her giggling.

The laughter halts when we all notice all the cars at my house. I know the silver car is Dom's; however, I don't who owns the black one.

I'm glad all the guys are here. It's time I told Kayne about Donovan. I should have told him this morning. I knew before I left what my decision would be. I have an amazing boyfriend, a wonderful family. I don't want to give all that up. Marco already stole five years of my life. I won't let Donovan rob me of anymore.

I'm getting stronger every day. The memories are there; they poke and probe at me when they realize I'm not listening to them. They demand attention, but with the help of Kayne and my family, my days are now filled with happy, loving moments that turn into good memories. They are slowly overtaking the ugly.

The good days wipe away the rawness of my nightmares. The more days that pass when I don't think about those painful memories, the less I remember how I felt. I know they were horrible times in my life and I recognize I will never forget them, but to be able to lessen the feelings associated with those moments is a possibility. I'm living proof, because every day another moment goes by, and I realize my days were filled with laughter, not tormented memories.

And with Kayne and Dr. Zeek's help, my confidence is building to great heights.

Lily gives Mom a quick hug from the front seat and exits the car.

I sit forward from the back, reach around and give her a big hug.

"Loved seeing my little girl smile and laugh today, Emmy." I lean back and smile at my mom.

"I'm happy, Mom, and I'm going to be okay." I give Mom a peck on the cheek and say, "Tell Dad I said hi and I love him."

My mom smiles huge, her eyes glassy with happy tears, and my heart expands to almost bursting knowing it's because of me.

I exit the car, Lily comes and stands beside me while we wave to my mom as she drives away.

We turn and begin walking to my front door.

"So whose black car do you think it is?" Lily asks.

I know what she's thinking. A black shiny car, almost exactly the same one Marco had in his empire.

"No idea, but I know what you're thinking."

"I can't see a black car anymore and not think about him," she whispers.

I reach out and hug Lily firmly. She gasps, surprised at my sudden comfort for her.

"Me too, but just like everything else, it will one day change as well."

I pull back and Lily stares at me for a moment and then smiles.

"I'm so happy you're doing well, Em. You deserve everything life has to offer. You have the bravest soul and the purest heart, just like my baby sister," Lily ends softly with a small smile.

That's a huge compliment and I'm going take it and try to live up to it for Lily, and for her sister Sasha.

We smile and walk up the porch stairs. I turn

the handle on the door and go to step through the entry. We don't get very far; the door is yanked from my hands and I have five sets of angry eyes staring at me.

Lily jumps back surprised, and I hear Jake curse and then he says, "Lil, come here, baby."

Lily goes straight to him. They embrace and he kisses her on the head. He then looks to me with a disappointed stare. I know that expression. I'm in trouble.

My eyes swing to Kayne and see his are furious, his lips pressed together and his jaw tight. He seems as if he can barely contain his anger at me.

What the hell is going on?

I glance left and find Dom and Nick are also looking at me unhappily. Dom's shaking his head at me, but it's the man next to them which has my eyes widening in shock. Joseph O'Connor.

Uh oh. Did Alexa tell him what we've been planning? No she wouldn't. Last I heard, she was hiding from Joseph.

Carefully and gently I say, "Someone want to tell me why I'm getting the evils from everyone and what he," I nod in Joseph's direction, "is doing in my home?"

Joseph's face softens at my words and his

expression turns apologetic. I didn't mean to be rude, but his presence is a shock. I know he was trapped just as much as I was and I know he helped free me, but why the hell is he in my house?

"We found your emails to Alexia," Kayne states; his tone is tight. He's trying very hard to restrain his anger.

Shit!

"I can explain—" I start, but Joseph cuts me off with a question.

"Do you know where she is?" His tone is slightly pleading.

"No, I only know she was in New York when we last spoke," I answer and he starts firing off more questions to me.

"How did you find her? Why are you both doing this? You know how dangerous that man is yet you have her following him."

The last is more like a statement than a question. His words hit me hard. He's right. This whole time Alexa has been in danger while doing what I asked her to do. I never once thought about her safety. I just wanted to know where Donovan was and it appears I would do that at any cost.

Disappointment seeps into my bones and my shoulders slump. That's not the kind person I want to be.

I step forward to get my laptop to tell her straight away to stop, to get away from Donovan now. However, Kayne steps in front of me like an angry bull, his breathing heavy and his eyes piercing mine with anger so visible I fear I might go up in flames.

"Answer the questions, Emily," Kayne clips to me.

Oh, God, he's furious and it's all directed at me. I deserve it. I should have told him sooner.

I stare into Kayne 's eyes as I say my next words, knowing they are going to hurt him. "Every time I saw her for my injuries, she would give me the same number. Saying if I escaped and needed help, to call her. I memorized the number. I had to see her a lot," I ended on a whisper, hoping Kayne didn't hear the last part.

Kayne 's expression twists into pain with my words and I know he heard it all. His muscles untighten and I watch the anger leave his body and his posture shows defeat. He moves back and sits on our stairs. Dropping his face to his hands, I hear his muffled, heavy breaths through his hands.

I step toward Kayne. "I was coming home to tell you everything."

Kayne gazes at me with a lost expression.

"I wanted revenge, and I still do, but I want to

find another way to achieve it. A safer way. I know going after him on my own is too dangerous. Please understand, revenge was all that kept me going some days."

Jake clears his throat and says, "Boys, let's take our plans to my place. We'll leave Em and Kayne to work this out alone."

I give my brother a small smile to thank him and he comes to me and gives me a tight hug. "I'm so mad at you, but I understand and I'm proud of you for realizing we can't lose you again, ever again." I nod into his chest and a few tears escape.

He lets me go and Lily gives me a quick hug and whispers in my ear, "It will all be okay. And next time, include me in your kickass girly revenge plan."

Jake notices my smile and narrows his eyes at Lily. She just shrugs and he looks to the ceiling and curses under his breath before they both leave.

Dom and Nick give me hugs next, nice warm brotherly hugs.

Dom whispers that he saw me smiling when I came in and says he's happy for me. He then instructs me to stop giving Kayne heart attacks.

Nick informs me of how incredibly dangerous I behaved. He gives me a soft kiss on my cheek and whispers, "Chin up, Em, things are looking up."

Dom and Nick leave together.

Joseph is the last to leave. His expression hints at the thousands of things he wants or is too scared to say to me. He leaves with a simple a chin lift and closes the front door.

The sound of the door closing echoes around the house and points out just how silent and awkward it is between Kayne and me at the moment.

"I'm sorry," I whisper into the room.

Kayne glances up from the ground to me and what I find in his eyes kills me. His face shows just how hurt he is. How hurt, sad and betrayed he feels.

"Just this morning you emailed Alexa back and said you would get back to her with your plans. I'm struggling here, Emmy. I don't understand how you could just this morning think about leaving me, disappearing again, and possibly never come back to me. Did you ever think about me? What I would go through when I found you gone. What I would go through if you fucking died!" he ends with a roar.

I step back, not because I'm afraid; I know Kayne would never hurt me. I move because of my aching heart and sickened stomach. I feel sick at how much I've hurt him with these simple actions and emails.

"I'm sorry. I'm so sorry. I did think of you. You are the only reason I didn't leave when I first received the email that *he* was in Mexico, you and my family. I wish you could understand how much I needed that back then, the possibility of revenge. This morning, the only thing that stopped me telling Alexa to stop and that I was telling you, was wanting to be there at *his* final moments. I know with you and Jake handling this, I will be as far away from *him* as possible. I thought I needed to see *him* go, see *him* suffer, but today, I realized I don't need that. Knowing he's gone will be enough because I have you all and that's all that matters. I won't let him take more years from me."

Kayne shakes his head and my stomach plummets as I see my words are having no effect on him. He's too hurt.

"I wish I could believe that. You've spent the last four months lying to me. The last two months telling me you were trying, and the last three weeks making me believe I had my Emmy back forever. Meanwhile, you've been planning on leaving to fight an impossible fight and knowing you would probably never make it back to me."

Tears prick my eyes as Kayne speaks the truth.

Kayne stands from the steps and I see his eyes are now glassy. "I have fought for you every day. I fight for us every day, and now I find out I was

229

fighting for nothing, for you to leave me when you found a way, a chance to get away unseen." He says the last few words with an incredulous tone.

I shake my head repeatedly while tears fall fast and thick from my eyes. "No, I mean, yes. No, argh, I was confused back then. I was lost and full of hate, Kayne. I thought finishing him, finishing what he started would help me move on. I know better now. I know the only way to move on was to let you in, let my family in and to accept the help I needed. You fought for us and won. I decided not to go after him. I'm fighting for us now. I was too weak back then, but I'm not now."

"You decided months too late, Emmy."

Kayne's words pierce my heart like no words have ever done before. What does he mean? And what does this mean for us?

Kayne steps to the table and picks up his car keys.

"I'm going to Jake's."

I freeze on the spot, that's it. He's just going to Jake's, no more talking about this.

Kayne walks to the back door and I hear him lock it. He walks straight past me without a glance and opens the front door. I grab hold of the handle to stop him from shutting the door on me and this conversation.

"Wait, I think we should work this out before you leave, Kayne. " I try to make my words come out strong but they appear more like a plea.

"I can't. I'm too angry." He stops and takes a big breath. "I just spent four years of my life searching for you. Dying on the inside without you, and you were just going to leave and put me through that again," Kayne says sadly, resigned. Is he giving up on me?

I slowly release the door handle as the fight in me dies. Kayne stares into my eyes for only a second longer before he closes the door in my face.

Tears slide out of my eyes and my heart constricts. Every fiber of my being is screaming at me to go after him, but he's right. What I did was wrong. I knew that though, all along.

Revenge played me like a fool.

Chapter Twenty-Three

It's ten pm and Kayne still isn't home yet. I received a text message from Lily two hours earlier telling me Kayne was still there with the guys, working on details for their travel to New York and finding Donovan.

I decide to text her and ask if they are still going. I'm anxious for him to come home. I need to make this right. I need him to know how sorry I am, how much he was the reason I never did leave to find Donovan on my own.

Hi Lil. Are they finished yet?

Five minutes go by before I get a reply.

Kayne, Dom and Nick left right after I text you earlier. I would have thought he would be home by now.

My heart grows heavy. Is he even coming home tonight? Is he staying with Dom and Nick? I can't just wait around to find out so I dial Kayne 's number.

It rings four times before I hear Kayne 's deep voice over the line.

"Emmy, everything okay?"

As I'm listening to him talk, I can also hear music and what sounds like a lot of people in the background. Where the hell is he?

"Where are you?" I ask straight out.

"I'm at Dugarel's bar, having a beer with Dom and Nick."

"So while I've been waiting for you to come home and wondering if you were coming home at all, you've been at a bar," I end on a hiss.

I'm pissed. I'm beyond pissed. I'm not even sure if I should be, I just know I am.

"Emmy, I just need some space, that's all. Time to think."

That word *space* scares me to death. *Worthless, used, pathetic.* Those toxic words roll around in my mind but I push them away. No, that's not what he thinks. They have nothing to do with who I am or this situation. I fight back the doubts and at the same time realize what he's doing.

"Yeah, I understand. I hurt you and you're trying to hurt me back."

"Emmy," Kayne whispers, his voice soft and

sad as if he's only just realized his actions have hurt me.

"Take all the space you need. Actually don't bother coming home tonight. Why don't you find some other woman who's perfect in every way and forget all about me."

I hang up the phone and stare at it. What did I just say? I close my eyes tightly. *Damn it, I didn't mean any of it.* I'm so mad at him for leaving me hanging over this argument.

The image of a razor appears in my mind and I take quick steps to the bathroom. On my way in, I grasp hold of the sides of the entry with a death grip. "Don't you dare do it, Emily," I say out loud to myself. "You've come so far. Don't ruin it. Be strong. If you do it now, every time after this will be harder and harder to stop yourself," I mutter firmly to myself.

I move away from the bathroom and sit on the bed. My pulse thunders under my skin. My breathing comes out in ragged gasps. *I don't need to cut. I am strong. I can get through this moment.*

This is just an argument. Couples have them all the time. This is normal; this is what I want. A normal life and a normal relationship where couples fight, because couples only fight as a result of caring so much about each other.

Ringing from my phone pulls me from my thoughts. I stand still and let the call ring out. I know it's Kayne. I'm not sure what else he thinks we have to say to each other.

It's rings again and this time I answer straight away. I want to hear Kayne 's voice. There's no use even pretending.

I say nothing and wait for Kayne to speak. This time I hear no music, no people, just the sounds of the outside and cars.

"Emmy," his voice is thick with emotion, but I'm not sure which one.

"I'm here," I whisper.

"Why did you do that? Just throw me away to someone else so easily. Years ago my Emmy would have stormed down here and dragged my ass home if she thought I was getting hit on."

"I didn't mean those words, Kayne. I'm angry and hurt. I wanted you to come home so we could work this out, together."

"And I want you to fight for us, Emily. I want you to want to be with me."

"I do!" I shout into the phone.

"Yeah, 'cause so far all I've seen is me fighting for us and you willing to leave me to get your revenge, and now you give me permission to go find some other pussy you know I don't want."

My eyes fill with tears. "I'm trying," I plead into the phone. "I'm trying so fucking hard, Kayne. " I sink to my knees, sobbing into the phone.

"Fuck!" Kayne shouts over the phone. "Emmy, baby, I know you are. Jesus, I'm just so fucking pissed at you. When I saw those emails today, they *killed* me. You may as well have put a knife through my heart because reading you were going to leave me, killed me, Emily. It fucking destroyed me."

"I fight for myself every second of every day. That means I fight for you, for us every second of the day. Please—" my words stall as my chest shudders through my tears. "Please understand, you mean *everything* to me."

"Fuck, I fucked up. I fucked up, baby. I'm coming home now. I'm sorry, Emmy." Kayne 's words come out strangled.

"I'll see you soon," I say softly.

Kayne curses into the phone right as the line goes dead.

I make my way downstairs and lie on the sofa to wait for Kayne. Only within a few seconds, sleep takes me.

***

I feel hands go under me and I'm being lifted. I open my sleepy eyes and see Kayne gazing down at me. His expression soft and his eyes apologetic.

He carries me upstairs in silence and I burrow into him, loving the sensation of his warmth. *Home.*

Instead of placing me on the bed, Kayne kicks off his shoes, sits on the bed and maneuvers his body backward, leaning against the headboard with me still in his arms. He adjusts his arms tighter around me and I find myself melting more into his body.

"Can you forgive me?" Kayne whispers into my hair.

"Can you forgive me?" I ask him back.

"Yes," he breathes out. "Promise me you will never leave me. That you will never put your life in danger."

"I promise," I pledge firmly.

Kayne sighs and it feels like he released the weight of the world from his shoulders.

"I was worried you might cut," Kayne says gently, his voice unsure.

I tilt my head back to meet his eyes. "I thought about it, but I stopped myself. I'm stronger now than I was before."

"Emmy," Kayne breathes out my name like a prayer, "I'm so proud of you."

I smile up at the love of my life and he gifts me with a soft, beautiful smile of his own.

Finally everything is out in the open and we can move on.

"Things are looking up for the not-so-doomed Romeo and Juliet," I joke.

Kayne 's soft smile turns into a blindingly bright one and he twists us on the bed until he's hovering over me. He tickles me under my arms, I laugh out loud, and snort as well. Our laughter echoes around the room. He stops and we gaze into each other's eyes, peace settles over me and a rightness in the world fills my soul. I'm staring at Kayne but in my mind I'm thanking God for sending me an angel of my own.

Chapter Twenty-Four

Giggling comes from the living room and I smile to myself as I place the remaining two slices of chocolate-iced vanilla cake that Sav and I made in the fridge.

I walk out of the kitchen and with an oomph, from a little person grabbing me around the legs, I peer down and see the sparkling brown eyes of my blonde-haired, gorgeous baby girl.

Giggling up at me, she says, "Daddy's tickling me to death." With a smile on her face, she says 'death' in a whisper like it's a huge secret.

Kneeling down to her, I kiss her on the cheek and she puts her soft five-year-old hands on my shoulders. I whisper in her ear, "Well, maybe Daddy needs to be tickled to death," She laughs and runs toward the sofa.

"Daddy, beware, Mommy and me are going to tickle YOU to death this time."

I watch as Kayne jumps from the sofa fast and shouts, "Ahhhh, no, not to death." He runs away from Sav, and I watch as they both run rings around the sofa. Giggling and a manly laugh intermingling into a beautiful song to my heart. The song of my family.

Kayne stops and turns on a laughing Savannah. She runs into his legs and proceeds to jump up and try to tickle him under the arms.

I enter into the huddle of laughter and tickling fingers. I give Kayne a push on his back and it takes him by surprise. He falls to the sofa with a bark of laughter. Then I climb on top, trying to pin his hands up above his head while telling Sav, "Quick, Sav, now, under the arms."

Kayne struggles with his hands and he's winning easily against me until Sav gets her tiny soft hands under his now clamped arm and lets out a loud boisterous laugh.

The poor man is so ticklish. If you can trap him while he's down, he's a goner. He can't handle it and just keeps laughing until he's out of breath. Which is what Sav means by 'death'.

Sav continues to tickle Kayne and I watch as his loud laughter goes silent. Yep, the man can't handle it at all.

"Okay, Mom, time to stop; he's dead,"

Savannah instructs.

I laugh loudly at my daughter and pull her up to sit in front of me on Kayne's chest. Kayne takes a few moments of deep breathing and then he finally calms down. Sav and I both stare down at him with huge grins on our faces.

Panting, Kayne says, "Now that's something I want to see every day, my two girls smiling down at me."

Sav jumps from my arms and Kayne's chest and stands next to us, pointing at Kayne. "I got you, Daddy. Bet you can't catch me."

With that she's off and running out the back door hoping her father chases after her so she can continue this game she loves so much.

Kayne looks up to me with a big smile on his face. Then his face changes to alarm, and I instantly understand why.

We both scramble off the sofa and run for the back door, and at the same time we yell, "Don't pull the roses out, Sav!"

A thump wakes me and I sit up in bed gasping for breath. I look to the sound and see it's the curtain on the window, thumping backwards and forwards with the wind. I look to the bed and find I'm alone.

I inhale and exhale deeply, unsure why I'm

panicked: the noise that woke me or the dream I just had? It's was beautiful. I had a daughter, a beautiful daughter who had mine and Kayne 's mixed features. She was absolutely the most beautiful thing I have ever seen.

I drop back down to the bed and stare at the ceiling for a few moments, going over every aspect of my dream. God, we were so happy. The little girl was so cheerful. She held no worry or concern on her face. She came to me for comfort, and I offered it easily.

One of my fears of having children is being able to protect them. How could I protect a child from the outside world when I couldn't protect myself? Or showing them beauty when I sometimes struggle to see the word that way.

But this dream, this little girl, she created the beauty. *Savannah.* My heart cries out for a little girl who isn't real. *But she could be.* Could I do it? Have a child and offer them everything they deserve. I know Kayne could, would, in a heartbeat.

I'm becoming stronger every day. This could be a real possibility. A family. I could still have my dreams; my future may not be dead after all.

I lie in bed for over an hour thinking of my dream and the little girl who has taken over my mind and heart in such a short time. I notice I don't hear Kayne moving around downstairs and realize he must have gone out. I throw the covers off me and spot a note on Kayne 's bedside table.

Didn't want to wake you, you looked like you were having a good dream. *Wink, wink.* It was about me, hey?

Gone to lunch at Applebee's with a friend. I'll be home in a couple of hours.

Lunch? I scan for the clock and find it's eleven am. Wow, I really did sleep in.

A friend? Must be one of the guys. But I can't wait. I want to tell Kayne now I've changed my mind; that I may want children. No, I do want children, one day. I want what was in my dream, for the both of us.

I'm in such a good mood. I dig around in my underwear draw for a push up bra I know is one of Kayne 's favorites. A soft pink, push up bra with frills. I grin to myself while putting it on. I can't wait until Kayne sees it when he's taking off my clothes later.

I pull on denim jeans and a blue drape tee. It's not low cut, but my push up bra has definitely lifted my boobs up high and they are pretty much saying hello to everyone. I laugh to myself because I can imagine this being the first thing Kayne 's eyes notice.

I race down stairs, put my sandals on, grab the keys and my bag, and lock the house up.

Ten minutes later, I'm driving into the restaurant parking lot. I park right next to the big Applebee's sign with a huge red apple on it. I spot Kayne 's truck and smile widely, happy he's still here.

I hop out with a huge grin on my face and my heart ready to burst with excitement. The more I think about my dream and what I'm going to say to Kayne, the more ecstatic I'm becoming.

Five months ago, this was never a possibility, feeling these emotions, smiling. The simple act of being excited. I'm so happy, ridiculously happy.

I practically skip to the door, and then I freeze as I'm passing the windows. I zero in on Kayne in the restaurant, laughing. With a woman. A woman I don't know and have never seen before. My heart picks up its pace and I tell myself to calm; there's an explanation for this.

I stare at them through the window and the woman laughs. I examine everything about her. Her light, thick blonde hair, almost white, is tied up into a high bun on her head. Her face is soft and inviting. She seems to be early thirties, Kayne 's age. She's wearing a black business dress with a black belt around the middle. I can easily tell she has acrylic nails as she waves them around while she speaks to Kayne. *My man.*

What's he doing having lunch with another woman when he told me he was having lunch with a friend?

I step back from the restaurant window, not wanting to be seen and feel even more of a fool if they see me staring at them.

Did Kayne realize I'm not worth fighting for? Did finding out about my hidden secrets yesterday finally push him away for good? *Worthless, used, pathetic.* I take slow steps toward my car staring at the ground, trying to make sense of this situation.

Friend, lunch, secrets, pathetic.

With a steel cased, heavy heart, I walk over to my car. My heart throwing itself around in my steel box, bruising itself, wanting to get out and go running to the man I love and claim what is rightfully mine.

I arrive at my car and stare into nothingness, thinking over the possibilities. Kayne came home last night. We talked and we made love.

There's no scenario in this world that the Kayne I know would turn to another woman five years ago and definitely not now.

But what if he saw how worthless you are?

No! Stop, those aren't my own thoughts; they

aren't my doubts. They were put there by an evil men who won't win. I won't let them take Kayne away from me. I need to fight. I need to do exactly what Kayne asked me to do last night. I need to fight for us. If I walk in there and find out my worst fears are true, then I'll walk away with my head held high. There's nothing wrong with me. I'm strong, a fighter, a survivor. I need to start being proud of myself, instead of hard on myself. That starts now.

I glare toward the restaurant with determined eyes. I'm going to fight for Kayne and fight for my dream. I damn well deserve it. I deserve what everyone else is able to have.

I storm across the parking lot, searching for Kayne through the glass and find him still sitting with the woman.

I throw open the restaurant door hard and walk through with purposeful strides. I step past the waiting area and straight to Kayne and the mysterious woman's table.

Kayne spots me and stands from the table quickly. Guilt written all over his features. My heart twists at seeing the guilt and what it could mean. Kayne starts to speak, but I extend my hand, palm up to us face, in a gesture that says stop. I turn to the woman and proceed to tell her exactly what is going to happen.

"Hi, my name is Emily. I don't know who you are, nor do I care, except for the fact, that you are having a secret lunch with my boyfriend. Now, you need to understand Kayne is not on the market; he's mine. So you need to take your fake nails and probably bleached hair and run along, now." I wave my hands in an off-you-go-now gesture.

She glances from Kayne to me with a confused expression.

"He's not going to help you."

I turn to Kayne while saying this and my next words stick in my throat as I observe the guilt is gone from his expression and now a grin is on his face. "So, so, just run—"

I narrow my eyes and I place my hands on my hips, not happy that he's smiling at a time like this. "What?"

"Emmy, meet Cassie, she's going to design you a photography studio. I was going to surprise you with it the day before construction started. But it looks like you caught me in the act," Kayne explains and puts his hand to his mouth in a fist to stop his bubbling laughter from escaping.

I'm frozen, staring at him, afraid to look at the woman I just insulted.

I raise my hands and cover my face in embarrassment. "Oh, my God," I say through my muffled hands.

Kayne lets out a laugh and pulls me into his arms. I wish I could just disappear into his body.

Instead, I turn to Cassie and breathe out a sincere, "I'm so sorry."

The woman is sitting back in her seat, not smiling, but not angry either. She's regarding me I think, so I decide to keep talking, well, rambling really.

"You see, this was my big moment. My moment to prove I will fight for my relationship with Kayne. " I point to the front of Applebee's. "I just had a major breakthrough out there. In. Applebee's. Parking lot." I speak each word carefully. "I never saw that coming!" I end with a hysterical laugh.

The woman's face finally shows some sort of expression. She smiles and stands; she extends her hand out to me. "Nice to meet you, Emily. I'm Cassie from Johnson Designers. I've heard so many wonderful things about you and your photos. I'm looking forward to designing the perfect studio for you."

My smile grows wider and I take her hand and shake it. "Me, too, Cassie."

"How about we reschedule this meeting for another time, Cassie, a time when you can come to the house and talk with both Emmy and me. I need to take this sassy woman of mine home, right now."

Kayne turns to pick up his wallet from the table and I glimpse him readjust his jeans. *Ooh.* I know what this means. I'm about to get lucky because I claimed my man and fought for us.

"No problems at all. Just call my receptionist and she will set up an appointment for you." Kayne and I nod and Cassie smiles as she leaves the table.

I slump down in her seat and stare up at Kayne. "I was such a bitch."

He grins back at me and says, "A fucking hot bitch. Don't get comfortable; ass in your car, now. After that claiming, I need to have you, hard and fast. Fuck, like right now."

The air grows intense, crackling with passion and need. My heart thumps wildly against my chest and my pussy throbs with the need to have Kayne inside me.

I jump from the table and Kayne takes my hand, leading me out of the restaurant, both of us walking quickly.

We arrive at my car and Kayne pushes me up against it, taking my mouth and grinding into me shamelessly with his hard cock, out in the open for anyone to see.

I kiss him back, just as eager. It's a furious,

lust-induced kiss. Our teeth clash as we try to be as close to each other as possible.

Kayne pulls back and we are both panting for breath.

"Home, baby, straight away. I have to drop some paperwork to the office for Nick but I'll be right behind you."

I nod and smile, knowing the next few hours are going to be bliss. Amazing sex and then explaining to Kayne I want to start a family with him. God, life is great. I can't believe I hid from it for so long.

Kayne slaps me on the ass as I turn to get in my car. I start the engine and drive out of the parking lot. I go left and I watch in my rear view mirror as Kayne goes right.

I turn the radio on and sing along with the music. My blood is pumping fast and my heart is bursting with love and happiness. My mind is full of only beautiful, mischievous thoughts. Ideas of what I'm going to do with Kayne all afternoon.

I'm almost home when my phone dings. I pull over to the side thinking it might be Kayne. However, I see the message is from Alexa and quickly open it.

Donovan is in Hastings. I followed him in last night, but lost him when he used a dummy to leave his hotel undetected. He knows Joseph is tracking him down, and I just got word; Donovan has eyes on you. He found you and he's following you.

Fear grips my heart. I drop the phone to the floor, my shaking fingers unable to hold it any longer. My trembling hands grip the steering wheel and I look around the area I'm stopped in. I notice a silver car about twenty meters behind me. It's parked. I can't see if anyone is in the car.

I fumble turning the key and the engine starts. I drive off rapidly with spinning wheels. I watch the silver car in my rear view mirror. It doesn't move. I'm far enough away where it's now only a speck of silver in the distance; it doesn't make a move to follow me. I blow out a breath. *You're freaking out, Emily. Just get home, lock the doors and tell Kayne when he gets home. You're safe. Kayne will protect you.*

At that exact moment, when those thoughts are caressing my mind, calming me, two parked black cars suddenly pull out in front of me, making a V, blocking my way forward. My heart jackhammers against my chest and my palms are sweaty and slipping from the steering wheel. I'm forced to brake and turn my car to the left. It slides until it comes to a full stop. I hear another car come up behind me and I turn around and see it's the same silver car from moments ago. *Shit!*

I hear a door open and turn back to the two

251

black sedans. And there he is. Donovan. He stands calmly and buttons up his gray suit jacket. He's wearing aviator glasses and I can't tell if he's looking at me.

My eyes are frozen on him as I hear a loud smash to my left and I scream as glass covers me. I bring my hands up to protect my face. A rough arm reaches past me to the keys and turns the car off.

I know if I lose those keys I lose my freedom. I grab for the man's huge hand and start trying to pull his fingers apart. I scream as loud as I can while using all my strength to pry the keys from him. He uses his free hand and places it around my throat, tightening painfully.

"Jesus, let go of my hand, bitch," he growls.

I keep going, clawing at his hands, and scratching at his skin. If he takes my keys, I'm dead anyway. Going back to that life, the cold, lonely, abusive place. I'd rather die right here by this stranger's hand.

"Christ's sake, Pete, just fucking knock her out and hurry up. We don't have all damn day," Donovan yells over to his goon. He shakes his head in annoyance and pins me with a stare through the window shield. "Emily, drop the fighter act. We all know how weak you really are."

The man squeezes my throat tighter and I'm

gagging through his hold, my screams becoming hoarser by the second. My fight wanes and I feel the old familiar feeling of helplessness and breathlessness wash over me as I drift into unconsciousness.

Chapter Twenty-Five

I reach home and I'm surprised when I don't see Emmy's car in the driveway. I can't have beaten her home. Wouldn't I have passed her? No, I came another way from the office. I jump out of my car, jog up the porch steps and try the front door handle and find it's still locked. I open it up, walk inside and call out for Emily.

"Emmy! You here!"

When I hear nothing, I pull my phone from my back pocket and dial her number. It rings out and goes to voicemail.

"It's Em, leave a message and I'll call you back when I can."

Beep.

My gut clenches; something's not right. Where would she have gone? I grab my keys to head back in the same direction Emily would have come from. I'm walking down the porch steps when I hear car tires screeching and then watch as Jake's SUV speeds down my driveway.

Joseph's in the front passenger seat, holding on tight to the roof while Jake brakes and the car skids sideways. Before the car has even stopped, Joseph is out and running up to me.

My stomach completely drops at this moment, the moment I know they're about to tell me what I already fear. Donovan has Emily and I wasn't there to protect her. I fist my hands waiting for the words which will destroy me.

Joseph reaches me breathing heavily, "Kayne, we found out Donovan is in Hastings and has eyes on Emily. We need to keep her out of sight. Don't let her go anywhere," he says, scanning the area around us and then turns back toward me when I don't say anything.

Joseph's confusion turns to fear, as what I'm guessing he's seeing is my whole body go pale. I lower my head and tighten my fists to where I know my knuckles are now white and my short fingernails are digging into my skin.

I sense Jake run up to us. "What are we doing standing around. Time to grab our shit and go kill a motherfucker." I hear his words drift off on the end and he asks, "Where's Em's car?"

I raise my head and growl, "He has her. Emmy

should have been home by now. She should have beaten me home easily. Fuck! He has her!" I end with a roar.

Jake's whole body goes stiff and he whispers, "No, not again. This can't be happening."

He takes two fast steps toward me, cuffs my collar and sneers into my face, "You were supposed to protect her. You were supposed to be keeping her in your sights. That's my baby sister, and if anything more happens to her, I'm going to hold you responsible."

I push Jake off me and roar, "I know! Fucking, fuck, fuck, motherfucking cunt! If he touches her again, I won't ever forgive myself!"

Jake and I face off, both with our chests rising and falling rapidly.

"Both of you shut the fuck up. If…" My eyes swing to Joseph and see him raise his hands in a maybe gesture. "If Donovan has her, he's still in Hastings. We have a real shot at finding him and getting Emily back. Stop the blame game. You both know even if you watched her twenty-four seven, at some point this fucker was going to get to her. He's obsessed with her. He was willing to wait you all out for as long as he needed to."

A ring sounds and we all look to our phones, but it's Joseph who speaks, "Holy shit. It's Alexia, she's calling me." He presses answer and turns the speaker on and says, "Lexi, where the fuck are you?" Disbelief still evident in his voice.

A feminine voice speaks through the phone, "I was on my way to Emily's house to warn her about Donovan, but now I'm heading east following three BMWs, two black, one silver. I passed them just before seeing a car matching the description of Emily's abandoned on the side of the road, driver's side window smashed. I turned around and caught up to the cars. You need to be on the road now and head east. I'll call back with an address when they make it to their destination."

"Like fuck. You turn around, right now, Lexi. Get the fuck out of there and out of this dangerous situation. I'm heading that way now. We'll find them."

"No," Alexa states firmly. From her tone, there will be no arguing with her.

"Jesus Christ!" Joseph yells out. "Do. Not. Stop. When they do, you keep driving and call me when you have a destination. Do you understand me, Lexi?"

"I'm going in after them. I'm not going to let them hurt her. I'm armed and ready to kill if they dare touch her."

"No!" Joseph shouts. "Don't, please, Lexi.

Leave it to us."

"I have to, Joey," Alexa says into the phone. "I didn't help her when I should have, at the beginning. I wouldn't be able to live with myself now if I drove straight past and did the same thing again. I would rather die then anyway."

Joseph looks up to me and Jake, begging for us to say something, but we both stay silent. If it was Lily or Emily, we would be saying the same thing as Joseph. But if she can save Emily, keep her from being taken away again, then I'm not saying a damn thing.

Joseph realizes what's plainly on my face. I'm willing to sacrifice Alexa to find Emily. He grinds his teeth and we watch as his jaw tightens. Then we all start running for Jake's truck.

We're in when Joseph speaks again. "Lexi," he breathes out her name. You can hear the defeat and pain in his voice.

Jake starts the car, revs the engine, and spins us around; we fishtail it out of my driveway. My home with Emmy. Please, God, let this still be *our* home, not my home again.

"We're on our way. Just don't do anything stupid, Lexi. I need you. I need you alive, baby."

As Joseph says the words we didn't think we would ever hear from a man as strong or brutal as him, the line goes dead.

Joseph roars into the back seat and throws his phone to the ground. He punches the back of my seat a few times, but I don't say anything. I completely understand. If I was a better man, I'd call Alexa back and tell her not to do it, not to try and save Emmy.

But I'm not a better man at the moment. I'm a desperate man.

I hear a dial tone and realize Jake's calling someone on speaker phone through the car. It feels as if I'm moving in slow motion, even though I can feel how fast we are driving.

"Smith, it's Jake. Emily's been taken, again," Jake growls into the car. "Put an APB out for the man we talked about earlier, Donovan Bradley. Shut down the airports closest to Hastings and have patrol cars out to the city's exits, right fucking now."

"On it." With that, Smith hangs up and we continue speeding along the road. Jordan Smith is the Lieutenant at Hasting Police Department. Jake must have called him earlier when he knew Donovan was in Hastings.

Emily's car comes into view. It's parked to the side on an angle. Jake slows when we pass and it's easy to see the smashed driver's side window.

"Fuck!" I roar into the car.

Jake revs his truck and we speed up Main Street through the middle of town and straight on to the back road, heading east. I know what's east. It's lots of abandoned houses, and Willow's Ridge Airfield.

If they secure her on a plane, I've lost her all over again. Emmy's come so far. How could she overcome any more hurt and pain? *She couldn't. She'll be lost to you.* I try to shake off the fear spreading through my mind.

I twist and turn in my seat, wanting to jump out and run to her. Wanting to do anything except sit still and pray we get there in time.

My heart is pounding in my ears. It's raging with anger that someone dare stole what is ours, yet again.

Chapter Twenty-Six

An ache in my neck is the first thing I feel when I wake. I realize it's because I'm sleeping sitting up. *What?* I swallow and my throat burns. I go to grab my throat with my fingers; however, my hands meet a hard, sticky resistance. I look down and see silver packing tape wrapped securely around both my wrists and ankles. I'm tied to a dirty, metal, dining chair.

Oh, God. Donovan. He found me. I'm caught. No!

My head shoots up and I examine my surroundings. I'm in a small living room with faded yellow walls and old, brown sofas. There is nothing else in the room except those old pieces of furniture and me, trapped to a chair.

It looks like nobody has lived here for a long time.

My eyes dart to the left as I see movement

outside the window. I swear I just saw long black hair run past the window.

"Ah, you're awake."

My head spins to Donovan, who is standing right in front of me. Dressed in his suit, he looks every bit of the gentlemen he isn't.

He kneels before me and lifts his hands to my face, but doesn't touch me. He just outlines the curves of my cheeks, close, but not touching.

"God, you become more beautiful every time I see you." I narrow my eyes and scrunch my nose up, hating that he likes me at all.

He laughs at my reaction.

"What's wrong, Emily, five months away from the collection and you suddenly don't fear me? I remember our last encounter; you were just a shell of a woman, no emotions or fears. Just a whore who opens her legs when told to."

I pierce him with my eyes, and resolutely state, "Not a whore, a rape victim."

Donovan's eyes widen minutely. Not enough to think I've shocked him, but enough to know he wasn't expecting me to have that kind of answer.

Two figures move into the room and stand behind Donovan.

"Donovan, we're heading out now."

Donovan speaks, but keeps his eyes and body facing my way. "Go, and take Pete. I want some *alone* time with Emily." His voice, dripped with honey, is disgusting. He smirks at me.

Shivers rack my body at hearing his words. My eyes dart around the room wildly. No, I won't let this happen again.

"Are you sure? What if—"

The man doesn't get any further in his sentence as Donovan stands, turns toward him and cuts him off. "Don't think, Jimmy. Just fucking do what I say," Donovan grinds out, his shoulders stiff and I can only imagine his face hard and angry. That expression has been directed toward me many times in the past.

The man shrugs and yells out, "Pete, you're coming with us." A third man comes into sight and they all leave through what I'm guessing is the front door.

Donovan turns back to me and I hiss, "I'm not going to let you touch me. Never again."

His mouth curves up into a sleazy, slimy grin and then as quick as a flash, his hand is on my right breast and he's squeezing it hard.

I scream out in agony as sharp, stabbing pains, radiate around my chest.

Donovan lets go and steps back.

Tears are escaping both my eyes and my face is scrunched up in pain.

"You're tied up, Emily. You can't stop me. Time to remind you just how worthless you are."

Fuck. Shit. God, please don't let this happen again.

I begin thrashing around in the chair. I refuse to let this happen. I refuse to be that woman again. This time, I *will* fight to the death, and if I die, at least I die with my soul intact and my heart full of love for the man I know who loves me, who loved me even at my weakest.

Donovan grasps the top of the chair in an attempt to stop me rocking it. He has an arm on either side of my face. He's laughing through his puffy breathes at trying to hold me steady.

"A lots changed in the last five months I see. Well, that just makes the next few months for me a lot more fun. I will beat this fight out of you."

All of sudden, Donovan's body spasms. His arms rock my chair. I'm frozen watching him. Then his hands fall away and his body slumps to the ground.

With him out of my way, I'm left staring at a woman I know all too well. Alexa Kingsley. She hasn't changed at all. Still a stunningly beautiful woman with long, black hair and a body most woman would kill for. She has a stun gun in her right hand and she's panting heavily. Fear evident in her features.

She drops the stun gun to the sofa and runs over to me, desperately trying to untie the tape around my wrists.

"I need a knife," Alexa says, more to herself than I think to me.

"The kitchen, there might be something in the kitchen you can use," I tell her and she moves quickly away.

I stare down at an unconscious Donovan as I listen to Alexa slamming cupboards and draws. She returns with a pair of rusty scissors and begins to cut through the tape. It takes a few minutes as the scissors are fairly blunt, but finally, she frees my right hand and has my left freed quickly. She bends and slices through the tape at my ankles.

Relief floods my veins as I jump up from the chair, rubbing my sore wrists.

I glare down at Donovan and realize I'm now the one in control.

"We need to get him in that chair and strap him to it. Did you see the tape they used on me in the kitchen?" Alexa nods and runs off to grab it.

When she returns, we lift a heavy Donovan into the chair. I hold his upper body steady by his shoulders from behind while Alexa tapes his ankles and knees to the chair. She moves on to his wrists, and when she's finished, I let go of his shoulders and we step back to look at him. However, the chair falls forward and Donovan's face smashes into the ground. He's too heavy.

Alexa and I stare down at Donovan thinking the whack to the face would have had to wake him up, but nothing; he doesn't move.

Alexa and I turn to each other and shrug. We left the chair upright again and tape around his chest to the back of the chair. Using the whole roll of tape, we're done and he's sitting upright. He isn't going anywhere.

I stare at him and a wave of intense power radiates through my body.

"The guys are on their way. They told me to tell them when I knew where you were, but I haven't yet," Alexa explains. I turn to her as she continues to speak, "I wanted to know what you wanted to do first. You can do what you wish with him now or I call the guys. They will come and deal with him. But you need to decide fast, because if they turn up, they are going to take us somewhere safe and you won't have this chance again. Donovan won't be leaving this house alive."

I stare back at Donovan, thinking over her

words.

"So what do you want to do?" she inquires.

"I want to hurt him. Make him bleed and scream," I reply.

She raises the rusty scissors in the air and says, "Time to wake an asshole up then."

I reach out and she slaps the scissors into my hand.

"But we can't be long. Donovan's guys will be back anytime and we need to let our guys know where we are before then."

I nod to her and move toward Donovan. I notice his fingers are lazily moving. He's waking up.

I twist the scissors around in my grip and place the handles together in my palm with the sharp end pointing down. I want to wake him up with pain. Yes, I want to hear him scream, right now. With that thought, I slam the scissors down into the back of his left hand.

The scream which rips from his mouth is intoxicating. It fills my veins and gives me purpose.

Donovan bucks in the chair, confusion written all over his face. His eyes roam the room crazily and then his gaze settles on me. His focus then goes to the pain and the scissors firmly planted in his hand.

"FUCK! You bitch!" His voice is guttural and I

spot tears seeping from his eyes.

I take a step forward and very slowly I pull the scissors out of his hand. A long, agonized scream bubbles up and out of Donovan.

My heart's pumping madly at seeing the red, sticky blood on the scissors.

I glance to Donovan and put my hand over my mouth in a fake, shocked expression.

"Oops, was that your hand? Is this your blood?" I point to the scissors with a grin on my face.

"You fucking bitch." His voice is low and shaky.

He glimpses Alexia, who is standing behind me. She shrugs and leans against the wall with a bored look on her face.

I smile and move to the other side of the chair and stare down at his other hand. Those big, vile hands that have strangled and bruised me so many times.

I raise my arm and Donovan shouts out in protest. "No, no, no, no, no. Argh!" as I plunge the scissors down into the back of his other hand.

I stand back and watch as Donovan thrashes around in the chair. His face cringing as the movement hurts his injured hands.

My body is buzzing with excitement and power.

I step forward and again, I slowly drag the scissors out. The tormented scream from his lips to my ears is magnificent and overwhelming. Hearing a person in pain does cause my soul to flinch, but knowing it's Donovan only drives the desire in me to do it again.

God, if he's in this much pain just from his hands, I can't wait until I reach his groin area.

Blood seeps from his hands, around his fingers and drips onto the carpet. Donovan bleeding before me, defenseless and weak. I'm searing this memory into my mind.

He lets out a crazy laugh and says, "You are fucked, Emily. Whatever you do to me, I will do to you tenfold when I'm out of this fucking chair," he ends in a frustrated yell, still thrashing around trying to free himself.

"You aren't leaving this house alive, let alone that chair, Donovan. You are the one who is *fucked*. Now, where should I stab you next? Ah, I know, your thighs, let's work our way up to your pathetic, disgusting dick shall we?"

Donovan tries in vain to lift the chair with his toes in order to get away from me. I laugh. It's a sound I've never heard come from me before. It actually reminds me of him. I freeze on the spot right before I stab his thigh and a little girl's giggle drifts through my mind.

I swear if I turned around, she would be standing right behind me.

My dream. My family. Could I still have that if I took a life? If I turn to the dark side for just a moment, would I be able ever to fully leave the dark, or would this moment follow me for the rest of my life?

I step back from Donovan and look around the room. A crushing weight hits my chest as I realize what I'm doing. This isn't me. This is him. This is what he does to people. This is what he did to me. He stripped me of my dignity and power and destroyed me. I won't let him turn me into a monster. I won't go down that road. He *will* die, but he won't take me with him.

Taking a life isn't something I can do. My soul already holds too many scars. I won't give it another. Killing, even someone like Donovan, isn't built into me. I won't be able to move on from something like that. He's tainted my life for too many years. I won't let him have another second.

I turn to Alexa and say, "Call the guys. Tell them where we are."

I drop the scissors to the ground and walk away from Donovan.

"You think he's coming for you. Your fucking boyfriend." He spits out the word boyfriend as if it's a bad taste in his mouth.

I move up next to Alexa as she begins to dial a number on her cell and we both turn around to face Donovan. How does he know about Kayne?

"He's not coming for you, ever. We received information they were headed for the airstrip. Where I knew all along they would go if I took you toward an airport. That's where my guys were going, to kill him and whoever is with him. Then no one can fucking follow me or you, Emily. No loose ends this time. I'm fucking smarter than Marco. Dumb fuck should have done this in the first place."

Alexa softly breathes out, "No."

I extend my hand and speak in a panicked voice. "Give me the phone, Alexia."

She quickly hands over her phone, and when she does, I can feel she's shaking. I tip my head up to her and notice the fear in her eyes.

"Joseph is with them?"

"Yes," she says softly and her eyes go glassy.

I hold her hand and state, "It's going to be okay. They can take care of themselves." My voice comes out strong; however, I'm not sure I completely believe my own words as my heart continues to pound against my chest.

I dial Kayne's number. It rings out only once before a panting Kayne answers, "Where are you,

Alexia?"

Thank God. My body instantly relaxes and I look up to Alexa with a smile on my face.

"Kayne, it's Emily."

"Emmy, baby. Fuck. Are you okay? Where are you?" he demands.

"I'm fine. Alexa is here and she helped me escape. Donovan is tied to a chair at the moment."

I peer up to Alexa with expected eyes and trail off to Kayne, "We are?" Alexa quickly answers for me loudly into the phone.

"We're in an abandoned house on the right side of the airstrip. Its yellow and the only one on the road. You can't miss it."

"Okay, girls, hang tight. We'll be there soon."

"Wait, Kayne!" I yell into the phone before he can hang up. "Donovan sent some guys to the airstrip for you all. They're trying to kill you. You need to be careful."

"I will, Emmy. Don't worry about me. We came prepared. Jake had everything we needed in the trunk of his car. They're on the other side of the strip looking through some warehouses. I haven't heard gunshots. I'll call them and we'll get out of here and come to you and Alexia."

I let out a big breath, feeling so much better

now having talked to Kayne.

"Okay, I love you, Kayne, please be careful," I beg. My words come out strangled as my lips tremble with relief.

"I love—" Kayne doesn't finish his sentence, as there is a loud bang and then an *oomph* from Kayne. "Ah, fuck. I've been hit. Fuck, Emmy, get out of the house, run and go with Alexa now. Leave and get somewhere safe!" Kayne shouts into the phone.

I'm frozen. Pure, undiluted fear has taken hold and my voice is too petrified to speak. My mouth won't move out of fear that time will shift to the next moment, reality will come slamming down onto me, and I will lose the impossible. Lose what I will never recover from. *I can't even think the possibility.*

I listen helplessly as the phone falls to the ground and Kayne continues to scream at me to run and find safety.

I flinch, my body recoils on the spot as I hear another gunshot and then nothing. Silence. No more shouts from Kayne.

"No!" My heartbroken scream booms around the small living room. That's all it does, bounce off the walls in sound waves. It doesn't save Kayne, and it can't save me.

Heavy footsteps come closer to the phone and

then the line goes dead. *Kayne!*

My knees are shaking violently. Unable to hold myself up, I fall to my knees. Silent tears sear down my face. Sobs are begging to be released, but I can't let them go. I want to be numb. I want this crippling agony and sorrow to dig a deep hole into my soul and never be released.

"What?" Alexa asks, her voice shaking. She shakes my shoulders roughly and screams, "Emily, what happened!"

"He's dead," I whisper.

Tears reach my lips and I lick the salty grief into my mouth.

Chapter Twenty-Seven

"Oh, my God," Alexa whispers and falls to the ground beside me.

My chest shutters and a sob explodes from my mouth and it fills the room.

Vaguely, I hear Alexa speak on the phone, yelling to Joseph to find Kayne and get out of there. She describes the house we are in, but it doesn't matter. I may as well be left sitting in this same spot until my dying day. Life will never be worth living now.

"What's that?" Alexa asks.

At her words, I focus my hearing and hear the ringing of a cell phone.

"That's my guy telling me if he's finished the job."

Donovan. I'd forgotten he was even here. His name is hissed in my mind, said with such hate that even I'm terrified for what he is about to go through.

I spring to my feet and go directly to where I hear the ringing coming from. It's in his pants pockets. I don't pause for even a second, my hand dives down into his pockets, and I pull out his vibrating phone.

What if Kayne 's still alive? What if he's just been shot and needs help. My heart races with hope. I swipe the screen and bring the phone to my ear.

I'm meet with heavy breathes, seconds of silence and then, "It's done." And then he hangs up.

Dead dial tone. Dead air. Dead Kayne. Dead heart.

Goddamn it, Emmy, will a day come when I can ever say no to you?

I clutch my chest where my breaking heart sits.

I love you, Em. One day, I'm going to a put a ring on your finger instead of a rose on your wrist.

A cry explodes from my lips.

Our life will be filled with smiles. We will be happy Emmy. Even if it fucking kills me, we will be. These are our dark day's baby, but they won't last forever.

My heart is begging me to stop, to block whatever is ripping through its just-healed flesh. It's crying. I'm crying. My soul is dying.

My mind wraps around my memories. Wrapping them up tightly, preparing to protect them. *Never forget.*

"Emily," Alexa whispers softly to me, my name escapes her trembling lips.

"Had to be done, Emily. I couldn't risk you getting away again, and this time it will be better. You will always be with me. No more waiting months to have our time together."

My body locks up. Indescribable rage sears through me. Not even when men took my body against my will, not even when I heard the screams of my friends while they were being beaten and raped did I feel this surge of madness. Never have I craved death and destruction this much.

I roll my hands into fists and find the cell still in my grasp. I squeeze my hand around it painfully, and then with a violent scream, I peg it at Donovan's head. It strikes him in the temple and he grunts in pain. Instantly, a gash opens on his temple and blood oozes out.

I spin around recklessly, searching for something else to smash on his head. I need destruction. I need to feel the chaos. Anything is better than this anguish.

Donovan laughs loudly into the room. The laughter is shrill and like nails on a chalkboard to my ears.

I grind my teeth together.

"Is this what I missed in the beginning? Is this how you started out in the collection? Damn, I missed some good times then."

His insane words barely penetrate my thoughts. My mind is too chaotic. Too many ways to torture and kill are running through my head.

"What's in your car, Alexia?" I demand.

"Wh-what?" Alexa asks confused.

I spin on her, not in the mood for wasting time and say impatiently, "Tools. Do you have any tools, guns, knives, or a jack hammer? Anything to fucking kill him with," I hiss and point to Donovan.

Alexa looks to Donovan then back to me and quickly nods. "Yes, I have a tool box in my trunk." As soon as Alexa finishes her sentence, she's jogging out of the house and to her car.

"You really think you can kill me? You couldn't do it before. What makes you think you can do it now?" Donovan asks in a smug voice.

I cringe at his hearing him speak. I can't tolerate his very existence, let alone hear his damn voice.

I pin him with a glare. "Before, I had something to live for. Before I had a future. Before I had the world at my feet. Now, I'm as good as dead and I'm taking you down with me." My voice drips with contempt for him.

Donovan pales. My emotionless tone and honest words break through his cocky persona and he finally realizes he is going to die in this room, with me, very soon.

The sound of a clanking toolbox is heard before Alexa walks back into the bare, ugly living room. A room that will be forever branded into my mind.

Alexa heaves it down onto the sofa and opens the lid. She moves back as I move forward to survey what tools she has. It's full of different types of screwdrivers, wrenches and other tools I don't even know names for.

I choose a blue screwdriver that's stained with grease and dirt. It looks old and blunt. *Perfect.*

I focus on Donovan who's looking at me with panic and fear on his ugly face. I slap the screw end of the tool into my hand a couple of times, taunting him.

"Where should I stab you first?" I inquire.

"My guys are going to be here any minute, Emily. You fucking stab me again with those or anything else, and I promise you, you will regret it when I have you tied down later," Donovan hisses at me.

That reminds me. I look back to Alexia. "You should go. Before his men do come back here."

She shakes her head. "No, I'm in this until the end. I should have helped you years ago and I didn't. This time I've got your back."

Alexia's words blow me away. She's guilty. That's why she's been helping me. She regrets being a part of Marco's empire. From what Lily has told me about Alexia, she was badly beaten for trying to help women escape.

I wish I had enough emotion left in me to care and tell her it's okay, that I forgive her. But I don't. Rage and revenge rules my direction. Not revenge for my lost five years, that seems so minuscule compared to a lifetime without Kayne.

I'm staring at the devil in the chair who has taken everything away from me.

Never again will I admire Kayne 's bright smile.

Never again will I hear his deep, husky laugh when he thinks I'm being adorable.

I imagine myself at a family barbecue, looking around the crowd of people hoping to see him, but knowing he's not there.

I see my rose garden in my mind and Kayne is there, standing in the middle, just staring at me.

I was supposed to have my first Christmas with

him again this year.

And the one thing I held in my grasp for a mere few hours. A family.

I dash my tears away roughly and wipe those thoughts from my mind.

My mind detaches from my body. The part of myself who doesn't want to do this, who could never do this to another human being.

I'm looking at Donovan but I'm only now just focusing on him. He's peering up at me like a wounded animal ready to flee. I step forward and he flinches. I smile. It's a sadistic, uncaring smile, one that takes great pleasure in his torment. This will probably be the last smile I make in my life. I decide it's time to get a few things off my chest.

I start speaking and I'm not sure if it's to Donovan or to myself. But these are words I feel I need to let go of, no matter who they are said to.

"I had moved on with my life. I finally realized all those years of abuse were because you hated yourself. Those name—worthless, used, and pathetic—they were all about you. It's how you see yourself."

Donovan narrows his eyes and his face darkens with rage. I'm hitting a nerve.

"I am strong, intelligent, and loved."

Donovan barks out a laugh, but before he can

281

speak I cut him off.

"That's why you've been obsessed with me all these years."

His eyes narrow at me, a tremulous wave of emotions flare through his eyes. His expression screams at me to stop talking. It's as if he's trying to will my mouth shut.

"You envied me. You saw me surviving through hell and you envied me. You wanted to be me. You wanted to be as strong as me. As intelligent as I am and you are desperate for someone to love you as much as I am loved. But you aren't me. You aren't strong. You aren't dumb, but you're definitely not smart either, Donovan. And number one, you aren't loved. You saw everything you wanted in me and you wanted to destroy me the way you had been destroyed. Or were you born like this and just wanted what you'd never had?"

"Fuck you!" he spits the words out in a shout. "You are as weak as I am."

"No! I was weak but not anymore. I figured you out. You could take my body as many times as you wanted, but we both know who the weak one really was."

Donovan lets out a laugh; it borders on anger and embarrassment. His laughter turns to high-pitched screams as I take the opportunity to surprise him and plunge the screw driver into his left thigh.

"Ahhh! You bitch! Fuuuck!" Tears flow down his face.

I stand back and leave the screwdriver firmly wedged in his leg.

"What's wrong, Donovan? You can't fucking hack it, can you?" His face changes from pained to realization at me saying his awful words back to him.

I pull the screwdriver out swiftly and just as fast, I push it into his other thigh. He screams all over again, but this time it's accompanied by begging.

"Ahhh! Fuck, please. Please stop! I promise I'll let you go. Just fucking stop."

His tears are coming fast and constant. His face contorted in pain and his eyes are clenched closed.

I thought I would enjoy his begging more. But I'd be lying if I said his pleas didn't affect me even just a little bit. *It's time to finish this.* I pull the screwdriver out and Donovan howls in agony. His face is pale and his eyes glass over; he's passing out.

Alexa gasps and I assume it's because of the blood now seeping down Donovan's legs. But then I hear it, the biggest joke God has ever played on me. Kayne's voice saying my name in my mind. Is this my punishment for taking a life? God plans on torturing me through it as well.

"Emily."

My world spins and the screwdriver falls from my hand. My blood stops pumping. My pulse unmoving. Then in a flash, I spin around and there he is. *Kayne.* My heart restarting sends a shock through my body, the current so severe I can't even get the scream out through my mouth. My body begins to shake, every inch of my skin spikes up with defiance to ward off the breakdown I'm about to have.

He's alive.

He steps toward me, but it's not his whispered, "Emmy," that breaks me, not the smell of his cologne or his blue eyes piercing mine. It's his touch. As soon as my flesh feels his, I succumb to the heartache, the devastation. I bend my body in on itself feeling all the pain I had just buried deep inside myself. It comes full force.

Kayne wraps me in his arms and we fall to the floor. I endure the spiralling emotions of loss, torment, and now, relief. I lost someone I can't live without and now he's here. He's touching me. He's alive and I don't know how to stop the pain and relief from entwining and wreaking havoc through my body.

Chapter Twenty-Eight

Kayne

Emmy is in my arms, her body shaking from her sobs. *My girl. I'm so sorry.* She's already been through so much. I wish she didn't have to go through this as well, but there was nothing else I could do.

"Baby, please stop, it's okay. I'm okay," I whisper into her ear.

She gazes up at me. My breath gets stolen as her agonized face and bloodshot eyes stare at me with awe. As if every word I speak is a miracle. I understand how she feels. It's exactly how I felt when we found her at Marco's house. The fear that at any minute you could wake up and realize this is all a dream.

"I'm so sorry you had to go through that, Emmy," I state gently.

She straightens her body and wipes the tears away from her face. In the process, she gets some of my blood on her face. I reach up and wipe it away and she looks to my hand and then to my leg.

"Oh, my God." Emily's voice is high pitched and panicked.

"It's okay. The bullet went clean, straight through, and I have a bandage on to stop the bleeding. This is just what I lost straight after I was shot."

Emmy regards me with wild eyes, scanning the rest of my body.

"I don't understand. I heard… I heard another shot. You stopped screaming and then the man…" Em stops and swallows hard. "The man said it was done." Her voice is achingly sad and her beautiful brown eyes show confusion.

"He did shoot me twice. Once in the leg another one in the chest. But the guys and I put on vests before we went in. You know Jake, he has this stuff as toys in the back of his car. When I realized he wasn't going to stop until I was dead, I decided to play dead. He bought it and left. Straight after, I heard gunshots. I got to my feet, made it out and found three dead bodies with Jake and Joseph standing over them."

Emily touches my chest, pushing up against my now vest-free abs. I wince and she pulls away instantly.

287

"No, no, it's okay, just a bruise where the bullet hit the vest that's all."

Her body visibly relaxes then she jumps up, her arms going around my neck and her mouth on mine. Hard and possessive. The kiss is wild, desperate, and so fucking hot. *That's my girl.*

"Shit."

At hearing Alexa curse, Emily and I both pull back at the same time and look to Alexia. Then come the thundering footsteps in the house. Joseph runs into the room. He looks around wildly and then pins Alexa with his eyes.

A deep growl emanates from his chest and he takes purposeful strides toward Alexia.

"Give me that goddamn mouth, Lexi."

Alexa looks like she's about to fall on her ass, but Joseph picks her up and Alexa wastes no time jumping into his arms and their mouths come together in a fierce, brutal kiss.

I sense Emmy turn her face to me and I gaze down into my girl's face. She gives me a small smile.

"Holy fuck," Joseph says and then places Alexa back on her feet. We watch as his body visibly relaxes. "Thank God, you're okay Lexi, but Christ, you are in so much fucking trouble. We have a lot to talk about." Alexa nods, agreeing with Joseph.

Jake comes bursting into the room, finds Emmy quickly, and takes quick steps to her. He picks her up and gives her a big hug.

"Em, fuck. Thank God." Jake's voice is strangled as he holds his sister tightly.

He glares at me with murder in his eyes, sweat dripping down his face. I grin because I know what he's about to say.

He points to me and says, "I'm going to kick your ass later for driving off and leaving me and Joseph behind. Do you know how far of a run that was?" he shouts at me over the top of Emily's head.

Groaning in the room suddenly gets all our attention and everyone shifts their heads to the bleeding motherfucker tied to the chair.

"Oh, I forgot he was still here," Emmy states.

I pull Emmy from Jake and inform her, "Time to go, baby. I'll deal with that piece of shit. You and Alexa are leaving now."

At that moment, we all hear sirens in the distance. All of us guys look at each other, knowing we don't have long to get this done.

"Jake, take the girls to the airstrip through the trees. Tell them you were hiding until help came. Tell Smith we found the girls and there was a shootout. I was shot and Joseph has taken me to the hospital."

"Emmy, when the police question you, tell them the three dead guys at the airstrip were the men who kidnapped you. Tell the police they took you to the airstrip and held you there until we arrived to save you. Tell them what I just told Jake and that's it. Don't mention Donovan. Smith is going to ask you if he was here. Tell him no. Do you understand Emily?"

Emmy nods, agreeing quickly. I see the determination in her face and the fight in her eyes.

"Joseph and I will take the cars when we're done here. Go."

Everyone starts moving. Joseph whispers something to Alexia. She nods and moves out of the room with Jake behind her. Emmy gives me a hard, closed-mouth kiss and then she's out the door following Jake.

Joseph and I look to each other. Joseph's smiling. It's a scary as shit evil grin. I don't smile, frown, or have any emotions about this moment. I just want this to be over with, once and for all so Emmy and I can finally move on. Knowing this man will cease to exist in the next few seconds, gives me all the peace I need.

Joseph and I move forward and stand in front of the motherfucker.

Donovan groans and then focuses on us

standing over him. His eyes widen and he says his last words on this earth, "Oh, fuck."

Chapter Twenty-Nine

It's been a week since *he* tried to take me. The week consisted of nightmares, but not of *him*. Only of a world without Kayne. Every day the emotions of those brutal moments hit me and I need to see or touch Kayne to chase away my fear. He understands and pulls me into his arms, holding me until the moment passes and my heart is reassured that he is here with me. The memories are diluting with each passing day.

The fear of knowing what it feels like to lose Kayne will forever stay with me. But that's life, isn't it? Taking the risk to love someone knowing one day you will lose each other. Love is pain. Without the pain, how would you know what love feels like?

Kayne hasn't mentioned *him* once since he arrived back with Joseph and I don't want to know. All that matters is we are safe.

My parents freaked out when they found out what had happened. Thankfully Jake and Kayne were able to calm them and explain the monster would never be a problem again. My parents understand what that meant and I know it gives them some semblance of peace.

Lily came over that night, rushed into my house, and knocked the wind out of me when she tackled me to the sofa, hugging me so tightly. I knew losing someone else in her life wasn't an option for Lily.

When she let me up, tears flowed down her smiling face as she spoke, "I missed all the fun of watching the bad guy get his karma."

She pouted. We then heard Jake curse behind us. "Jesus Christ."

We both burst out laughing and Lily said, "High five, sista. You kicked ass." We high fived and then a flash went off. We looked over and caught Kayne holding my camera.

He shrugged, saying, "Now you can add your picture to the others, Emmy."

He walked out of the room and I was left staring at the spot he just left. My picture would join the other photos of people who are smiling, happy.

A picture of me smiling.

Kayne had my smiling picture blown up and framed. At the moment, it's in the dining room on the wall, but it will be moved into my studio once the construction is done. The other pictures of our family and friends have been framed as well, added to our wall in the living room. The rest of the pictures I have put away, somewhere safe. They may be pictures of strangers, but they represent a time in my life when I struggled but held on. When I fought through every day the best I could. They represent me surviving.

***

One week later.

I gaze up at the blue sky, the breeze rolling over my body. I'm lying on the pebbled trail in my rose garden. I inhale the fresh, beautiful smells of my roses. Reaching over, I caress a pink rose, stroke the petals, and appreciate the softness.

I remember the belief I held not long ago that the only time my life or I would ever be perfect was before my abduction. That I could never get back that carefree, loving girl that Kayne put a rose on for my prom. My rose and that moment in time became my obsession. Instead of looking at what I had, I kept looking at what I thought I had lost. But examining this rose now and seeing the edges darkening, the leaves bent and the petals ripped in places, I now understand that even roses can't be perfect. They all have their own scars from their life cycle, yet they stand tall and are beautiful.

I am a rose. I have scars from my life, but I am strong. I stand tall and I grasp life every day and live. I survived. I'm a survivor and I'm proud of myself.

I hear the creak of the back door opening and watch as Kayne strides toward me.

"My girl enjoying her rose garden?" he asks.

I smile up at him. Bending, he scoops me up into his arms. I squeal at the surprise and then wrap my legs around his waist.

"There is one thing I've been dying to do again in this rose garden," Kayne states with a wicked grin.

He swiftly places us both on the ground in the middle of the rose garden, next to the fountain. I'm surrounded by the warmth of the man who never gave up on me. I stare into his eyes and hope he can see the everlasting love I hold for him. Kayne places soft kisses along my jaw, while I stare at the beautiful, flawed roses, and the sun shines down on us. We make love in the rose garden and I let go of my skewed, perfect, existence and embrace my flawed, wonderful, and precious life.

Epilogue

Three months later.

Today, Kayne and I are having a barbecue at our house with family and friends. He thinks I woke up this morning and just wanted to have a barbecue just because, but I have a surprise for him. I'm going to surprise my whole family.

I glance around the yard and smile. It looks beautiful. Kayne hung fairy lights around the trees, the fence, and our back porch. He really went all out for just a barbecue, which is a bonus for me because it means when I surprise him, it will be in a beautiful atmosphere and most importantly, at our home.

I'm in a group with Lily, Jake and some friends of ours talking. I touch my back pocket and feel for my surprise. A smile graces my lips as I think about how shocked and happy I know Kayne is going to be. It's almost time.

I search the crowd for Kayne and my eyes land

on Alexia. She's laughing with Nick. It's the fake 'I'm giggling so hard because I'm hurt' laugh. and Joseph weren't around during the week after the attempted kidnapping. However, Joseph came to see me before he left for his uncle's house in Mexico.

"Emily, there are no words I can ever say to you to right my father's wrongs. But I want you to know, I will do everything in my power to make sure my family never touches you or your family again."

I asked Joseph not to go. I told him it wasn't up to him to right what his father did or what his uncle may do. We all urged him to stay here, with us, and start a new life. But he was determined to leave.

Alexa was heartbroken. She begged him to stay. She pleaded with him right on our front porch.

"Joey, once before you chose to stay at your father's to help Jake. I understood that. I wanted to leave so badly, but I understood you wanting to help him. Now, I'm begging you. Choose me. Stay here and forget that life. Start a new one with me."

"Lexi, I can't just sit back and let my uncle keep digging into my father's death. If he finds the answers, they are going to lead him right here."

"There isn't anyone left but us, Joey," Alexa says frustrated. *"Everyone else is dead. There's no one to tell him anything."*

"No, I'll go. See what I can find out and

hopefully stop him from starting what my father created."

"And me? I'm supposed to wait around again. Wait to see if you come out alive? Once you enter that world again, Joey, you won't be able to escape it."

"I will, Lexi. I'll come back. I promise."

Joseph steps to Alexa but she moves away from him shaking her head with tears trickling down her face.

"No, you need to choose. You stay here with me or you go to your uncles, but if you go, we are done. Forever done. I won't ever want to see you again." Alexa's chin quivers on her last words.

"Lexi," Joseph whispers. "I need to do this," he says softly.

Alexa gasps out in shock. Joseph isn't choosing her. I can see the pain on her face that even threatening their relationship isn't changing his mind.

"You need it more than you want me?" Alexa asks, her voice painfully sad and her tears coming fast and heavy.

I go to move to her, to comfort her, but Kayne doesn't release me from his arms and shakes his head sadly at me.

Joseph says nothing. He just stands and stares

at Alexia. The torment of what he's doing to her is written across his face.

"I'll be back for you, Lexi, no matter if you want me in your life or not. I'll be close by." Joseph walks down our porch steps toward his car.

A loud, brutal cry comes from Alexa and then she screams, "I hate you, Joseph O'Connor! You're just like your father, an uncaring monster!"

After Alexa lands those hurtful words, she spins and races into the house.

Joseph's face goes pale and his shoulders slump. It's the first time I've seen him look truly defeated.

He gets into his car and drives off.

I look up to Kayne with glassy eyes. "He's making a huge mistake."

Kayne kisses my temple and says, "I know, baby, but that's for him to figure out and hopefully, not before it's too late."

That was six weeks ago. The guys had been receiving secret phone calls from Joseph for two weeks. Kayne said he was just checking up on Alexa and letting the guys know everything was going fine at his uncle's.

Then the calls stopped. They've tried to find him, but it's as if he's disappeared. *Dead maybe.* I shake the thought from my mind. We haven't told

Alexa anything. All she knows is, Joseph left her here alone and she is on a one-way street of heartache. She goes out a lot, drinking, meeting new guys. Pretending she's okay when it's clear she's in so much pain.

I understand now how everyone saw right through me. When you care about someone, you notice these things. You care if they are happy or sad.

Suddenly, the lights go out and the backyard glows with just the fairy lights. I look around, confused, and everyone grows silent. Then I hear my name.

"Emmy, where's my girl?"

I step through the crowd and find Kayne standing in the middle of my rose garden. He's changed from shorts and a polo shirt into black slacks and a light blue collared shirt. He looks devastatingly handsome.

"Come here, Emmy." He motions me with his hands.

My palms instantly sweat and my heart jumps around my chest at his gesture.

I walk toward Kayne, the boy I love so deeply and the man I will always cherish. Kayne's grin is cheeky and it lights up his whole face.

I come to a stop in front of him and straight

away, he gets down on one knee.

Tears swim in my eyes, blissfully happy tears.

"Emmy, I've considered you mine since the first moment we met and I saw you had the face of an angel. Then I fell harder when you showed me your loving, carefree nature. Life has tested us, and we have survived our dark days. Now it's time to live in the light and have our happily ever after."

Kayne lifts a small ring box from the ground. He opens it toward me and in it sits a beautiful diamond ring.

"Will you marry me, Emmy?"

Inexpressible joy flows through my body. My heart and stomach in a flurry at how to express how happy I am. I don't think there are words or actions to show what I'm feeling right now, just my happy tears and my smile on my face.

"Yes!" I shout so everyone and the whole world can hear that I'm going to marry my best friend, my lover, and my savior.

All around us our family and friends clap and cheer, yelling out their congratulations.

Kayne places the diamond on my ring finger and gazes at me with a brilliant, handsome grin. He tips his head down and kisses me while his warm hands tenderly stroke my cheeks. He kisses me gently, as if it's our first kiss. Kayne moves his

301

hands from my face to my waist and pulls me closer. One of my happy tears falls to my chest and then I remember that this moment is about to get even better.

I pull back. Kayne 's smile distracts me for only a moment before I say softly to him, "I have a surprise for you too."

His features show a small amount of curiosity and then he grins mischievously at me. "Oh, yeah, a surprise I'm going to get later on, when everyone is gone." He waggles his eyebrows and I burst out laughing.

"This is something I can share now," I explain.

Kayne doesn't say anything he faithfully watches me with a mix of confusion and excitement.

I pull the positive test out of my back pocket and hand it to Kayne. When he realizes what he's holding he inhales sharply. "Emmy," he breathes my name out in shock.

"I'm pregnant, Kayne. " I softly say to him. "I'm five weeks. I took the test this morning. I missed my last period and I felt off the last few days so I decided to take the test. I stopped taking my pill two months ago. I wanted to tell you so badly but I wanted to surprise you more when it actually happened. I smile up at Kayne, but all I see on his features is still confusion and worry.

"Emmy, I thought you said—" I stop him before he can finish the sentence.

"I know what I said. I was lost and hurting then." I grasp Kayne 's face between my hands and look him right in the eyes. "That day I came to Applebee's to find you; I did that because I had the most beautiful dream of us and a little girl. She was our daughter and our lives were amazing. Filled with love and a special girl whose giggles still float through my mind to this day. I was coming to tell you I wanted a family." I place my hand on my stomach. "You loved me at my weakest. Now trust me at my strongest. I want this."

I watch as tears escape from Kayne 's eyes. "I'm so fucking happy." His voice is thick with emotion. "If it's a girl, let's call her Rose."

Warmth radiates through my body and my heart soars to unreachable heights. "Yes," I reply, as many more happy tears continue to fall.

Kayne takes my mouth quick and hard before releasing me and yelling out to the whole back yard, "We're having a baby!"

Everyone gasps and begins cheering. My mother's squeals of delight being the loudest. She races over to me and shakes my shoulders while tears cascade down her beautiful face.

Surrounded by our family and friends, who are congratulating us, my heart is close to bursting. I look around and admire what my life is now, and I'm blown away. So thankful I never gave up, even in my darkest days, this is what I was fighting for.

I search for my big brother and I find him standing on the outside of the crowd, holding Lily in his arms, both of them smiling at me. The two people in the world, other than Kayne, who know what this moment truly means to me. I smile at them and then look to the heavens.

I am Emily Roberts.

I am a survivor.

I am happy.

I am loved, greatly.

YOU LOVED ME

You Loved My At my Darkest (Lily and Jake)

You Loved Me At My Weakest (Emily and Kayne)

You Loved Me At My Ugliest (Alexa and Joseph)

PORTLAND STREET KINGS

Collision (Slater and Piper)

Fatal (Mack and Lana) – Coming 2016

Tail (Della and Dom) – Coming 2016

Pursue (Kelso and Ivy) – Coming 2016

Drifting (Pacer and Sophie) – Coming 2016

Book #3 is available now.

YOU LOVED ME AT MY UGLIEST

Joseph and Alexa's story.

Acknowledgements

To **my husband**. - Thank you! You keep believing in me and knowing that makes me so incredibly happy. I think if I said I wanted to become an astronaut you would tell me I could do it. You would probably mail off my application to NASA for me. xx

To my parents, Sarah, Mel and Amber – Setting goals and achieving them is what drives me to keep going. That feeling of accomplishment and confidence that fills me when I know I completed something that did have doubts circling when I first started. Those doubts lessen with your words of encouragement and confidence in me. I'm not sure if you all know how crucial you are to my success, but you are a massive part of how I get to my goals. When I was struggling with YLMAMW I thought I might have to move on and then I got an email from my Dad. We talked about my release date and how I was going. I said "Hopefully I can do it." My Dad replied with, "I know you will." That moment was one of not wanting to let him or myself down and one where it was that simple, he knew I would finish this story. I reflected back to that email a lot during writing YLMAMW, it was probably the only reason I was able to push through my struggles with Emily's story and finish. Thank you **Dad**, I love you.

To **TGFR ladies.** - I've seen a lot in this community in such a short time of being a part of it. You ladies showed me that even though there are people out there to tear you down there are also many more to help build you up. Your advice, friendships and knowing I have people to turn to when it all gets too much, means the world to me.

To my Betas, **Amber**, **Bel**, **Gill** & **Mandy**. - Thank you for reading my story and putting your lives on hold to help me. Each of you gave me an enormous amount of help and guidance and I thank you all for that.

To **Evie's Collection**. – Thank you all so much for your daily support, laughs and encouragement. A BIG thanks to **Elizabeth, Jolanda, Rhiannon, Jennifer & Jeneane** for continuing to share my covers, teasers and posts. Means a lot to me ladies.

xx

About The Author

Evie is an Australian author whose passion for reading lead her into writing. Evie spends her days writing heartbreaking, suspense filled love stories with happily ever afters. Evies characters are strong alphas with even stronger heroines who bring sexy sass to the relationship.